MARKED FOR VENGEANCE

SUSAN HAYES

Marked For Vengeance (Book 6 of the Crashed and Claimed series)

First Print Publication: November 2024

Editor: Amanda Brown

Cover Art: Croco Designs

Published by: Black Scroll Publications Ltd

This book is dedicated to my parents, for all the love and support they give their 'weird' daughter.
This is also dedicated to my Koala - my very own romance hero.

ABOUT THIS BOOK

She thought she was too old for adventure... until it blew up her ship.

Protecting her client while they cruised around the galaxy was easy work—at least until all hell broke loose. Now Loris is stuck on a hostile planet with poisonous flora, dangerous fauna, and a cocky-as-hell alien with big horns, broad shoulders, and an ego the size of a planet.

She needs to do her job. He's decided she needs *him*. The longer they're together, the more she wonders if he might be right...or if she's losing her mind as well as her heart.

***Buckle up. This sci-fi romance contains an alien with fur, fangs, horns, and a very possessive attitude when it comes to the woman he's claimed for his own.*

1

———

THE *BOUNTIFUL HARVEST* was not a small vessel, but most of the space inside its hull was dedicated to keeping its passengers alive. While Loris appreciated that, she still wished the ship's designers had found a way to increase the size of the passenger areas without compromising their ability to survive in the hostile environment of the void.

She was currently wedged into a corner of what she'd learned was the largest of the cabins. In fact, it was the captain's quarters. Captain Perez had offered it to Maddison as soon as she'd come aboard.

One thing Loris had learned in her years working for Maddison was that wealth came with more perks than she'd ever imagined. Of course, no one knew that Maddison wasn't wealthy anymore. When her marriage contract to Donny Cappa expired, the bastard had made sure she received her payment in the most disadvantageous form he could manage. Maddison Summers was the new owner of an interstellar matchmaking cruise service that had been profitable once.

These days, it was something else entirely.

Maddison set down the tablet she'd been reviewing and sighed. "These contracts can't be enforceable. What they're offering isn't legal anywhere in the known systems."

They'd been over all this before, but Loris nodded along. Maddison was more than a client. She was a friend—one who needed a moment to vent her frustration and horror at what she'd discovered.

The *Bountiful Harvest* reminded Loris of herself. The ship had been impressive once, but she wasn't young anymore. Her appearance was dated, her systems needed constant maintenance, and even some of the crew referred to her as the "old girl" when the passengers were out of earshot.

The ship *Harvest* wasn't past her prime yet, but that day was coming. Loris shifted in discomfort, though the pang she felt wasn't a physical thing. It was the knowledge that she was reaching the end of an era. Soon, she'd be too old to be a bodyguard anymore. Maddison's safety would become someone else's responsibility, and she would do... *what?* Retirement sounded like death by boredom to her.

Maddi was one of the few people whose company she truly enjoyed , and the rest were either dead or had fallen out of contact over the years. As for romantic options... She snorted in derision at the thought. She'd been too tall, too strong, and too plain-spoken to attract a guy when she was young and nominally pretty. Now she looked exactly like the woman she was—an aging combat veteran with no tolerance for bullshit and eyes that had seen too much death.

"You're doing it again," Maddison said.

Loris shrugged and pretended she had no idea what her friend meant. "What?"

"You're listening to the wrong voices."

She shook her head and barked a rueful laugh that held more emotion than she'd intended to show. Loris tapped a finger against her temple. "I'm alone in here. No voices of any kind."

They both knew that wasn't true. As their professional relationship had morphed into a close friendship, they'd shared a few late nights of introspection, deep thoughts, and self-doubts. Not to mention an unwise quantity of alcohol. Maddi's husband was a bastard of the first order, but his liquor cabinet was stocked with the finest of everything imaginable.

"You're too hard on yourself." Maddison flashed her a gentle smile. How the woman had managed to survive her time with Donny and still hold on to her humanity was a mystery to Loris. If she'd found herself in Maddison's situation, she'd have murdered the man a dozen times over, and none of the deaths would have been quick or merciful.

Despite being Maddison's bodyguard, she hadn't been able to protect her friend from her contracted spouse... and Loris's employer. The end of the marriage contract had freed both of them from Donny's control.

Her hands tightened into fists as she reflected on the past. If she ever set eyes on that man again...

Maddison rose from her seat, laughing softly. It took her only two steps to be close enough to rest her hand on Loris's shoulder. "I know that look. You're thinking about my former husband."

Since the contract ended, Maddison never used his name. She claimed it was because it invoked unhappy memories. Loris believed that, but she also thought there was more to it—a superstition of sorts, as if speaking the asshole's name might somehow summon him across the galaxy.

Loris snorted and grinned at her friend. "I imagined what his face would look like if we launched him out of an airlock and into the void. You should try it sometime. It's cheaper than therapy."

Maddison clicked her tongue in disapproval, but her eyes sparkled with amusement. "You know I love you, but it still worries me that you have moments where you sound like a psychopath."

"I'm not a psycho. I'm a soldier. There's a difference."

Maddison lifted one brow but said nothing.

"There is. When I choose violence, it's because I'm protecting someone or something I value. A client. An ideal..." She reached up to pat Maddison's hand. "Or a friend."

"I hope you never have to make that choice again. At least, not for me. I want nothing but a calm, quiet life where I can do something that matters." Maddison removed her hand and then looked around her small cabin. "I think this company has potential. It could be exactly what I need. The personnel can stay, for the most part, but everything else needs an update. Including this ship."

The one thing Loris had noticed about the ship was her crew. All of them seemed competent, and many of them were openly empathetic to their passengers, doing all they could to make their time on board memorable. That had been true when they'd come aboard, and it was still true now that a good portion of the passengers had departed to start new lives.

Some of them had found legitimate connections. Others made loveless but still beneficial arrangements, but there had been whispers that some of the arrangements were little more than breeding contracts. That's why Maddison had quietly requested logs and documents from previous trips. She'd wanted to know the truth, and it was even uglier than she'd expected.

"I hope so. It would be nice to think that romance isn't entirely gone from the galaxy. Who knows," she joked. "Once you've gotten this company sorted out, maybe you'll find a nice fellow who falls madly in love with the owner."

A shadow passed over Maddi's face. "I doubt that's in the cards for me. But I have every intention of using this matchmaking business to find someone worthy of you."

Loris barked out a laugh. "Me? Stars no. I'm quite happy on my own, thank you. Love is for other people. The ones with kindness in their hearts and hope in their souls. You know damned well I have neither of those things." She believed every word she said, but some small part of her wished it wasn't true. Loris pushed that thought back into the shadowed corners of her mind.

"You are one of the kindest—" Maddison's compliment was cut short as all hell broke loose. The deck beneath their feet lurched, and a heartbeat later, alarms blared from every speaker, both inside and outside the cabin.

Shit.

"Go bag. Now. Get it and meet me at my cabin door. Move!" Loris was at the door by the time the last word left her mouth. She hated leaving Maddison, but she needed to grab her own bag. At least her cabin was only across the corridor and a few meters down. She sprinted the entire distance, wincing at the noise and flashing emergency lights. Not good. Not good at all.

2

Vengeance loped through the forest of their adopted home world, leaping over obstacles as he followed his clan-brother, Risk. None of them had been in this area before, so there were no trails or markers to follow, but they knew where they were going.

More or less.

The strange ship had crashed before their rudimentary tracking system could manage more than a rough estimate of its location, but it was enough. They would find the ship and its precious cargo of unclaimed females. At least, Vengeance hoped they were still unclaimed. Most of the clan would have already arrived by now, and his brothers might have taken all the females for themselves.

He growled in frustration and picked up the pace. Why were they moving so *slowly?*

"Faster," he snarled to no one in particular.

"Remember what the female said," Havoc growled back. "We need to be gentle with these humans."

"If any are left by the time we reach them," Vengeance snarled. "We're moving too slowly."

Risk glanced back over his shoulder, his fangs bared. "Would you like to lead for a while, Venge? You can set whatever pace you like. If you're away from Havoc, maybe the two of you will stop arguing."

"I'm not arguing," Vengeance stated. He'd been trying to make Havoc see reason. The stubborn male was always forming complicated plans to achieve simple goals. Vengeance didn't see the point.

Risk stopped and spun around to face him, his expression a blend of bemusement and frustration. "You're *both* arguing. One of you wants to rush in. The other wants to make elaborate plans and consider every possible scenario. You're wrong."

Havoc stopped immediately—probably because he'd been moving so *slowly*. Vengeance took several more strides to come to a halt. Risk rarely spoke out like this. Of all their brothers, he had the most self-control. Vengeance was the opposite, especially when it came to spending time with his brothers. None of them found it easy to be with the others for more than a few hours. Instinct drove them to aggression and acts of dominance that strained their bonds and made it impossible for them to live in any kind of close community.

The three of them had been together for too long— first on the hunting trip and then on this journey to the crash site. Vengeance considered that for a moment and grudgingly admitted to himself that maybe he had been arguing with his brother. *Maybe.*

"We can't both be wrong," Vengeance said.

"Yeah, you can." Risk thumped a fist to his bare chest. "*My* plan is the right one."

Another plan? Vengeance groaned inwardly. Why was any of this necessary? They knew everything they needed to do.

Two days ago, the verexi's automated defense systems had shot down a ship with human females aboard. Several escape pods had ejected before the main vessel had made what they all hoped was a survivable crash landing.

Since then, three of their brothers had located pods and claimed the females they found for themselves.

Once the others learned of this, the rest of the clan had rushed to the crash site to find any survivors. Only Bysshe had stayed behind. The android was the closest thing they had to a father figure, but while he was a clan-brother in spirit, he had no need for female companionship. At least Vengeance didn't think he did. Did Bysshe even have the parts for sex?

He backed away from that line of thought before it led him somewhere no one wanted to go. Bysshe didn't talk about what he was or what he'd done before the verexi had bought him and put him to work as head keeper for their most dangerous experiments—the fa'rel.

The three of them were out hunting when news of the females broke. They'd arrived hours after the others had left to find the crashed ship. His bastard brothers hadn't bothered to wait. Which he couldn't really blame them for. He'd have done the same thing in their position, but he was still going to be pissed about it. It was the same for his brethren who had found mates. Sure, he was happy for Mayhem, Strife, and Menace, but he was also racked with envy. He wanted what they had—not their females, of course, but one of his own. Someone he could talk to about things his brothers would never understand. A companion to fill the long, empty nights when memories of his past haunted him. A mate to warm his bed and explore all the ways they could pleasure each other.

Thinking about it made him even more certain his idea was the right one. All these plans were unnecessary. Vengeance's sense of smell was better than any of his brothers, but he hadn't realized how much better it was until now. None of them seemed to have noticed that Hope and Menace's scents contained nearly identical elements. It wasn't that they smelled the same, but their scents complemented each other in ways he couldn't explain.

That had always been his problem. His instincts provided him with information, but he struggled to put the knowledge into words. Bysshe had tried to teach him the science behind his ability, but Vengeance could never stay still and focused long enough to absorb it all.

"And what's your plan?" Havoc asked. The question jerked Vengeance back to the present moment.

"Nice of you to finally ask," Risk said.

The note of rebuke in his brother's tone made him wince a little. In all the time he and Havoc had argued, Risk had kept silent. Vengeance had assumed he agreed with Havoc simply because that's how it usually went. They all thought of Vengeance as the reckless one who always charged in. They weren't entirely wrong about that, but they weren't right, either. He operated best when he let his instincts guide him.

Vengeance bowed his head and waited for Risk to speak. It was as close as any of them got to apologizing. Havoc did the same.

After a moment, Risk spoke again. "We have no idea how any of this mating crap works. We've never *seen* a female before today. Assuming there are any survivors, don't you think we should get to know them before we decide we want to spend forever with one?" He pointed at Vengeance. "You want to charge in and claim one, but what if she doesn't like you? What if you don't like her?"

Vengeance considered explaining what he'd noticed about Hope and Menace's scents, but he couldn't find the words. Instead, he shrugged. "You think that could happen?"

Havoc scratched his beard, considering things. Then he scowled at Risk and said, "When did you become the logical one?"

Risk scoffed. "Right after the two of you saw Menace's female and lost your fucking minds."

Vengeance snarled in resentment. He hadn't lost his mind. Meeting Hope had simply made him even more determined to reach the downed ship and try to find a female whose scent matched his own.

"But she was so beautiful," Havoc said.

Annoyance with the delay and constant chatter pushed him to action. Vengeance turned and shoved his clan-brother hard enough to make Havoc stumble. "Hope is pretty. My mate will be *beautiful*," he declared. "I will claim the best of them for myself."

Risk snapped. "That's not what Hope said. She told us to be gentle with the females. Remember?"

"No," Vengeance lied. He recalled every word the little human female had uttered, but he didn't want to admit it right now. "I don't remember that part."

"She said to be gentle, like Menace was with her." Havoc swung his head from side to side and grinned a little. "I don't think that word translated correctly. Our brother is far from gentle."

They all laughed in agreement. Menace was more like him than many of his clan-mates. Whatever the verexi had done to them, the results had not been uniform. Each of his brothers had their own talents and temperaments. Vengeance had never understood why they'd created the fa'rel to be so different from each other when their creators valued conformity. From the clothes they wore to the way they spoke, everything about that race was the same.

After the laughter died away, Risk spoke again. "Hope also said that if we were lucky, one of the females might choose to bond with us. *Might*," he repeated. "We shouldn't assume we can simply lay claim to one of the females."

Vengeance growled, not in disagreement but because he knew how right his brother was. They wouldn't be able to lay claim to whatever female they found. She had to be the right female for them. But if he was the only one who knew that, would the others try to take a female who wasn't the right match? If she were among the survivors, would any of his brothers try to take *his* female? They needed to catch up before that happened.

"I like my plan better," was all he said.

Havoc turned and shoved him. "You would. Simple minds like simple plans. Risk is saying I'm right. We need a plan."

Risk raised his voice. "That's not what I said!"

Frustration and anger flowed off him in waves, triggering an instinctive response from both him and Havoc. Vengeance's fur stood on end, and his hands curled into fists at his sides.

Havoc snarled and raised one hand, his claws extended and his teeth bared.

No one moved. This always happened when they spent too much time with other members of their clan. The wrong word or a sudden move was all it took for a fight to break out, and that would only delay them *more*.

Determined to break the standoff, Vengeance forced himself to relax as he unslung the pack from his shoulders and started rummaging around inside it. "If we're going to stand around here for a while, I'm eating. You two do whatever it is you're doing."

The tactic worked. The others relaxed, and the charged feeling in the air dissipated like when mist met a stiff breeze.

In no time, the three were eating and talking as if the entire incident had never happened.

Risk talked the most. He explained what he thought needed to happen. He wanted to act faster than Havoc did, with a flexible plan that would allow for more variables, but he still seemed to want to complicate things more than Vengeance liked. It sounded like a compromise, which meant no one got what they wanted.

When Risk was done, they lapsed into a thoughtful silence. No one agreed to anything, and now they had three ideas for how to proceed instead of two. That might be a problem later, but none of them seemed too concerned about it now. It was how things worked. Every member of the clan had the freedom to make their own decisions, so long as their choices didn't threaten the safety of the others. After a lifetime of experiments and imprisonment, the right to make their own choices was too important. He and his brothers would fight to the death before they allowed anyone to take their freedom again.

Once they were underway once more, something did go Vengeance's way. Risk set a faster pace than before. Soon they were racing each other through the woods, their tawny coloring allowing them to blend into the gold and orange foliage. Every step they took before nightfall reduced the distance they'd need to cross when the sun rose again. Even with the shortcut they'd taken, they were still nearly a half-day's journey from the area of the crash site. Their clan-brothers would be there soon. They might have arrived already, depending on how fast they had traveled. If he'd been with them, they'd have raced the entire way.

Vengeance shot an annoyed look at Havoc. If Havoc still led them, they'd probably be walking. He wiped the expression from his face almost as quickly as it appeared. As annoying as his brother's approach could be, sometimes he was right. Havoc had been one of the planners who orchestrated their escape from the verexi.

The fucking scrawnies had lied to them. They'd

convinced the fa'rel that the entire experiment was a failure. That part was true enough. While he and his brethren were lethal warriors, they were also stubborn and resentful of any attempts to command or control them.

Their captors told them they'd found a suitable planet for the entire group, and they'd be allowed to live there unmolested. *That* was all a lie.

The scrawnies wanted them dead and blasted into atoms to get rid of any proof they'd ever existed.

He and his brothers had other ideas. Havoc and several others worked with Bysshe to find a way to break out of the cargo hold they'd been trapped in. They'd battled the droids on board, forced their way through sealed bulkheads, and taken control of the ship. Of course, none of them had any idea how to fly the fucking thing, so they'd ended up crashing onto the surface of the planet.

It was still better than what the verexi intended to happen. The damned scrawnies still wanted them dead and sent mercenaries to the surface periodically to try and exterminate them. They'd killed so many that Vengeance suspected the local wildlife had developed a taste for anything in armor.

It was a good thing none of the fa'rel wore any.

3

———

It only took a few seconds for Loris to open the door to her cabin and grab her bag from inside. Years in the military had drilled into her to always be prepared for shit to go sideways, and she hadn't dropped the habit, despite the fact she'd been a civilian for nearly fifteen years.

By the time she was back in the corridor, Maddison stood waiting, her own pack slung over her shoulders. "We're going to the bridge. I need to know what happened, and it's the safest place I can think of."

She grabbed Maddison's arm and took off at a jog. The deck lurched, lights flickered, and with every few strides the ship uttered low, tortured groans or sharp creaking noises that made her increase speed.

At least they weren't in the passenger area. Loris could imagine the chaos that must be unfolding on the lower decks. Scared civilians leaving their cabins, clogging up the corridors, unsure where to go or what to do.

They were still a few steps away from their destination when new alarms rang out. Over the noise, she heard the captain call for all off-duty crew to report to the bridge.

Shit. Shit. Shit.

Once they reached the door, Loris watched her friend's back while she tried to input the passcode. It took her several tries and a long string of curses, but Maddison eventually got it open. They raced inside, the door sliding shut behind them.

Maddison spoke first. "What's happening?"

Captain Perez shot them both a grim look and pointed to an empty chair. "Sit down, strap in, and shut up. I'll explain if we live through the next few minutes."

Maddison glanced at Loris, who nodded.

Once Maddison was secured, Loris took up a position behind her, one hand firmly gripping the back of the seat.

The deck bucked again, and this time the lights flickered and died. The emergency lighting kicked in almost immediately, bathing the bridge in a reddish glow that only added to the sense of foreboding.

Time passed slowly while every member of the bridge crew worked furiously, their eyes locked on their screens and hands flying over the controls. Loris couldn't make out any details, but she didn't have to. The ship was in trouble. She kept expecting the door to open and more of the crew to arrive, but it stayed closed. If none of the crew were able to make it here, hull breaches or sealed hatches had to be in their way.

Captain Jodi Perez's voice broke the silence.

"How many escape pods deployed?"

"Six deployed. But those bastards have shot down three of them," a crewman named Hooper replied. The woman was ashen, her hands closing into fists as she slammed them down on her console.

"We're sitting ducks out here! We're going to die."

Captain Perez shot her a stern look. "Keep it together, Hooper. We're not dead yet."

The pilot called out a moment later. "Ma'am, we have another problem. We're falling into the gravity well of a planet, and we only have partial power to our normal engines."

"Fuck!" the captain yelled. It took only a second for her to recover. "Joy, get me everything you can about that planet. Atmosphere, survivability. Can we breathe the air if we go down?"

"Yes, ma'am." Joy wasn't part of the bridge crew, and Loris was surprised to see her at a station. Why was the ship's guest liaison officer here?

The question went unasked. Now wasn't the time. Not when the ship was coming apart around them. At least, that's what it felt and sounded like to Loris.

Captain Perez bowed her head in defeat as she opened the ship-wide comms again. "This is the captain. I'm ordering everyone to abandon ship. I repeat. Abandon ship."

She turned to look at Maddison. "That includes the two of you."

"I should stay," Maddison argued.

"No, ma'am. You need to board the command shuttle. Once we're inside the atmosphere, the autopilot can handle the descent and landing on its own."

"Where do we go?" Loris asked, already scanning the area. She needed to get Maddison out of here. Now.

"That hatch over there." Jodi pointed out the spot and then turned her attention to the one called Joy. "Bashir, you go with them and see to their safety. I'm counting on you."

Joy nodded crisply and unclipped her safety harness.

Loris barely got two steps before things started to unravel.

Crewman Hooper protested, "What the hell, Captain? You're sending the blind party planner? What can she do to protect the VIPs?" Loris realized the other woman was already unclipped as she got to her feet, looking wide-eyed and ready to bolt. "I'll do it."

"Hooper! You will sit your ass down right now. Your place is here, ensuring we do everything possible to bring this ship down intact."

Loris led Maddison, keeping her body between her client and the unstable crewman. Out of the corner of her eye, she saw Joy Bashir attempt to join them without drawing attention to herself.

She failed.

Hooper—Loris belatedly remembered that the woman was the first officer on board—uttered a wild, broken sound and threw herself at Joy. The smaller woman went flying, arms flung out as she tried to regain her balance. Her head hit the deck with a thud that made Loris wince. She didn't need to look closely to know that Bashir was down and out of the fight.

Loris dropped her bag and charged at the first officer before the other woman had time to recover. Her unexpected takedown of Bashir was ugly and out of control, leaving her vulnerable. Loris took full advantage of the opening. The bridge wasn't large, but it allowed her enough room to accelerate a few steps before she stretched out one arm and used it to clothesline the out-of-control crewman.

Hooper made a horrific gurgling noise and clutched at her throat. Her eyes went wide and her mouth gaped open as she struggled to breathe.

Loris turned and lashed out with one foot, striking the already injured officer in the back of her knee and sending her toppling to the deck. She hadn't heard anything, but she'd felt the way the joint gave way and knew Hooper wouldn't be getting up again. Not with her knee shattered. She might survive her fractured larynx if she got immediate medical treatment, but something told her Captain Perez wouldn't make that a priority. Not when the ship was going down.

"Take Bashir and get out of here!" Perez barked at Loris.

"On our way." Loris took a second to straighten and give the captain a sharp salute, her fist clenched and held by her right cheek. "Good luck, Captain."

The captain nodded once and then moved to take over the first officer's now empty chair. No one even glanced at Hooper.

With no time left, Loris hurried over to the still unconscious Joy Bashir and grabbed her under her arms. "Maddison, get inside the shuttle and start emergency departure protocols. I'll be right there."

Maddison was visibly shaken, but she vanished

through the hatch without question. Loris had taught the woman how to perform basic flight checks and emergency procedures long ago. She had no doubt they'd be on their way in no time at all, which was good because the faster they got clear of the doomed ship, the better their chances of survival were.

At least in the short term. Getting away from the *Harvest* was one thing. Making a go of it once they were down on the planet's surface was another thing entirely. She didn't even know where the hell they were, and she had no time to ask.

The shuttle was larger than she'd expected, which was nice. She managed to wrestle the still unconscious Bashir onto a bench and strap her in. Then she made her way to the cockpit. Maddison gave up the pilot's seat immediately. "We're almost ready to go. I waited for you to start the final sequence."

"Good job." Loris dropped into the newly vacated seat and assessed the controls. Nothing unexpected. In fact, it was older technology, similar to what she'd learned to fly during her military service.

"Strap in and take a deep breath. We made it through the first challenge."

Maddison smiled tightly as she fastened her safety harness. "That *challenge* represents the loss of everything that son of a bitch gave me in the divorce. It's all gone, Loris. The ship. The business..." She sobbed softly. "The people. Oh gods, Loris. Are they all going to die?"

She considered lying but then decided not to bother. Maddi wasn't stupid. She knew the answer already. "Some of them will. But Captain Perez and her crew are good at their jobs. Trust them to take care of everyone still on board." She tapped in the command to launch. "Everyone but that bitch Hooper."

They broke away from the main ship. For one glorious moment, everything was calm. No more alarms. No flashing lights. Loris exhaled a long breath.

Then the shuttle was plunged into chaos as atmospheric entry tore at the little ship. She reacted instantly, attempting to alter course to improve their angle, but the controls stopped responding.

"What the fuck?" she shouted in frustration.

Then a thought occurred. "Ship. Can you respond?"

"Yes." The voice was flat, artificial, and indifferent. "What is your query?"

"Why can't I use the controls?" she demanded.

"No registered pilot is on board. All systems have reverted to automatic control."

Maddison gasped.

Loris cursed to herself. "Override requested. I am a qualified pilot."

"Negative. No registered pilot is on board. Emergency protocols have been activated."

"At least tell me where we're going?" she snapped.

"This shuttle will descend to the planet below. Name unknown."

"And what system is this planet in?" Surely this fucking machine had some information.

"Current location confirmed. System name unknown. Planet name is unknown." It spewed a series of coordinates Loris couldn't understand. Astro-navigation was beyond her understanding.

"Simplify it for me. Whose territory are we in?"

"This shuttle is two hundred light years from its expected course. All territory in this sector is claimed by the verexi."

Maddi uttered a small, fearful sound and gripped her hands in her lap.

Loris bit back another litany of curses. How the fuck had they wound up in the territory of the most unpleasant, xenophobic, and fiercely territorial species in the galaxy? The *Harvest* shouldn't have come anywhere near their region of space.

This shitshow couldn't get any worse. Could it?

She was afraid the answer was yes.

4

THE THICK FOREST and heavy underbrush gave way to new terrain as they reached the first rise of hills. Vengeance caught glimpses of the sky more often, and the ground was open and easier to traverse. Vengeance upped his pace yet again, despite the fact they were now headed uphill.

Tomorrow's trek would suck harder than a black hole. They'd have to hike up the mountains to reach the far side and the crash site. There was an easier route, but his brothers had taken that one. This way was faster.

The sky was darkening with the first signs of twilight sooner than he wanted. As much as he wished they could press on, they couldn't risk moving at night. It would be too easy to injure themselves in the unfamiliar terrain or cross paths with a predator they hadn't seen before.

They'd have to make camp soon. The thought rankled him despite all the reasons it had to be this way. He wanted to keep going. His mood soured as resentment churned in his soul. He flexed his hands as he ran, extending his claws in time to his stride.

Only the view helped him to stay in control. The sky was full of color, the golden light so thick he thought he might be able to reach up and carve out a piece of it to keep for himself. The forest below stretched out like a river of fire, the yellow and orange foliage adding to the illusion.

In the back of his mind, he started to compose lyrics to describe it all. It was something he'd always done, though he'd never admit it to his brothers. His music was a private thing, a way to find solace in the suffering he'd endured before they'd finally escaped to this beautiful but dangerous planet.

Thoughts of danger made him wonder how the survivors would fare. He hoped they were smart enough to protect themselves until his brothers arrived. As lovely as Hope had been, he had sensed she was far too gentle to survive for long on her own. Would the other females be like her? Probably. He'd never met anyone like that before. The verexi were cruel, distant, and often afraid of their creations. His brothers were loud, proud, and fierce. Bysshe was... Vengeance paused. Bysshe was Bysshe. Firm. Wise. Steadfast.

What kind of person would his female be? If there was one for him. If they weren't too late already. If any female would ever look at him the way Hope had looked at Menace... with adoration and not a hint of fear.

Havoc slowed and then stopped. A second later he pointed to a spot above them. "Tell me that's what I think it is."

Vengeance stopped to look and saw it immediately. Metal gleaming in the light, a symmetrical object too perfect to be natural. "A ship!"

"It's some kind of vessel," Havoc agreed, "but how long has it been there? Bysshe said they only saw three escape pods on the scans, and this isn't anywhere near where the big ship went down."

Vengeance heard the hesitation in his brother's tone. Oh no. Not again. No more plans! "You're too fucking cautious," he growled.

"And you're both too focused on finding females. It's a ship. That means possible supplies and salvage," Risk said.

Havoc barked out a short laugh. "You're hoping it can still fly. Aren't you?"

Risk tugged on one of his horns and shrugged. "Maybe. We should still check it out." Then he turned and pointed at Vengeance.

"But slowly. If females are around, charging in there will scare them. Especially if yours is the first face they see."

Vengeance feigned indignation even though he knew it was a joke. "You calling me ugly?"

Havoc laughed. "Not ugly, my brother. Terrifying."

"That's better." Then he spun on his heel and sprinted toward the ship. They could stay and make plans if they wanted to. He intended to scout out the vessel... and any females that might be on board.

"What happened to slow?" Risk called after him.

He didn't bother answering. The time for talking was over.

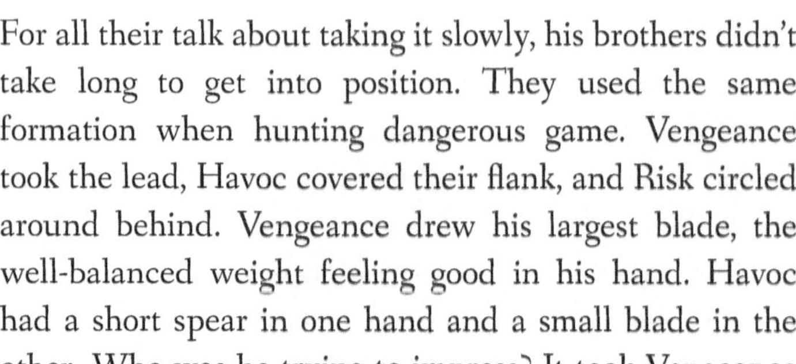

For all their talk about taking it slowly, his brothers didn't take long to get into position. They used the same formation when hunting dangerous game. Vengeance took the lead, Havoc covered their flank, and Risk circled around behind. Vengeance drew his largest blade, the well-balanced weight feeling good in his hand. Havoc had a short spear in one hand and a small blade in the other. Who was he trying to impress? It took Vengeance only a second to answer his own question. *Females.*

It wasn't until the wind shifted that he finally caught the scent the others had already detected. *Food.* Several meals were involved, each with a unique scent profile. There were proteins he didn't recognize, some familiar seasonings, and a chemical smell that stung his nose. The food might be strange, but that scent told him the meals were prepackaged and made to last a long time. The scrawnies had provided something similar on the journey to their new home. They could be emergency rations or the kind of thing soldiers consumed when out in the field. He'd have to get closer to know which it was.

A minute later, he knew. The evening breeze strengthened, carrying new information to his sensitive nose. There were three of them. At least one was armed with some kind of energy weapon.

There.

He broke into a jog the second he sensed it—a scent he'd only encountered once before when he'd met Hope. All three of the new arrivals carried the same scent markers, probably something to do with the ship they'd all traveled on together. The ship full of human females.

In a matter of seconds he was through the tree line and into a clearing. Two strides forward were all he managed before an energy pulse slammed into the ground nearby.

"That's far enough," a female voice rang out. Steady, clear, and full of authority.

For the first time in his life, Vengeance didn't mind being told what to do. He froze and tried to keep from grinning. They'd found females!

He could see two of them. Both were in the entryway to the ship, one standing with the other lying prone at her feet. The prone one had a blaster trained on Risk, who had just stepped into view. Vengeance ignored her. All his attention was on the female aiming a pulse rifle at him. She had a warrior's confidence and enough skill to know how to use the hull of the ship as partial cover. Admirable. Her short hair was the color of clouds on a summer day, and her eyes were a deep shade of green.

His cock stirred as the wind carried her scent to him, and it told him all he needed to know. She was *his*.

5

Despite the unknown threats, the loss of the *Harvest*, and everything else that had happened, Loris had to admit things weren't all bad.

Against all odds, the autopilot had set them down in a decent location. In fact, it was downright scenic. The sky was a dazzling blue, and the foliage ranged from soft golds and umber to blazing shades of yellow, orange, and red.

The shuttle was stocked with plenty of prepackaged foods and a decent supply of recyclable water, and so far, none of them had seen any kind of wildlife that could be deemed dangerous.

Loris already knew that Maddison was resilient and had her own brand of quiet courage, but Joy Bashir proved herself to be an excellent and good-natured companion who was more than capable. No wonder the captain had put her in the shuttle with them.

They'd treated her concussion with some of the more advanced meds in the first aid kit and left the more minor injuries to heal on their own. She still had headaches, and one ankle was sprained badly enough she couldn't do much besides limp around the interior of the shuttle. She made up for her lack of mobility by doing most of the meal prep and answering their questions about what had happened to the *Harvest* before they'd arrived on the bridge.

Nothing she told them was good news. Not only did she confirm they were inside verexi space, but the ship hadn't only suffered a mechanical failure that knocked it out of hyperspace. Someone, most likely the verexi, had fired on the *Bountiful Harvest*. Entire sections of the ship had been exposed to the void, crippling her and ensuring they had no way to escape the gravity well of the planet.

They'd received no word from the *Harvest* since the incident. All they could do was hope the ship had managed to stay relatively intact on the way down so at least some of the passengers and crew had survived.

They'd spent some of their time together learning about Joy's blindness. The story was familiar enough. She'd lost her sight in an industrial accident caused by poor maintenance and a disregard for the safety of the workers. Her eyes looked natural enough Loris hadn't realized she was blind, especially since she acted like a sighted person. It turned out the headband she wore collected visual data and sent it to her visual cortex, allowing her to "see."

Joy hadn't said anything, but Loris suspected the headband had been damaged during the fight with Hooper, probably when Joy had struck her head on the deck. Joy could still see well enough to get by, and none of them had any chance of repairing the delicate medical device.

They'd set up a simple camp, and once that was done, they'd told stories and shared details of their lives. They couldn't do much else to pass the time while they waited for someone to respond to their rescue beacon. According to Joy, this planet was uninhabited.

As the sun dipped down toward the horizon, Loris and the others discovered that Joy was wrong.

Loris didn't know what sense had told her they weren't alone anymore, but when the feeling came, she'd reacted instantly. "Maddi, into the shuttle and lie down on the floor. You know the drill. Joy, stay where you are. I'm coming to you."

Maddison raced up the ramp, only slowing enough to step around Joy, who was in her usual spot by the shuttle door.

Loris rose from her place by their small campfire and joined Joy on the ramp, grabbing a pulse rifle for herself and handing a blaster to the woman now stretched out along the floor with most of her body out of the line of fire. For someone with limited experience, the woman had learned the basics with impressive speed.

Something big moved beyond the tree line, its true shape hidden in the shadows that formed as evening fell. When she finally saw it, she nearly put a hole in its chest out of instinct. Her finger was already tensed on the trigger when she registered that despite its size and bestial appearance, this was no wild animal. The new arrival walked on two legs and had human-like facial features, but she had no idea what species it was.

Golden fur with subtle color shifts that acted like natural camouflage covered his body. Dark stripes spanned his forehead from eyebrow to hairline, and long blond hair fell to his broad and damn impressive shoulders. Oh yes, this had to be a male.

He strode deeper into their camp, and Loris squeezed off a warning shot, sending a pulse of energy to slam into the ground at his feet. "That's far enough."

The big alien whatever-it-was stopped, but he didn't lower the blade he carried. Instead he gave her a long, slow look that made her stomach flip. Most of her was hidden behind the shuttle's hull, so why did she feel like he was mentally undressing her right now? He couldn't even *see* her. Could he?

Another male moved into view. This one had a blade in one hand and a spear in the other, and he was a slightly smaller than the first she'd seen. Both of them were clearly in their prime with hard bodies and predators' grace.

Gods save her. Was she ogling them? What the hell was wrong with her? With a mental head shake, she got back to the business at hand. "Do you understand me?"

"We do," one said. "We have translators. I'm Havoc." He tilted his head toward the larger male. "That's Vengeance. You must be from the *Bountiful Harvest*."

She hissed in shock at the mention of the *Harvest*. "How the fuck does he know that?"

She didn't notice she had spoken aloud until Joy answered her. "Ask him."

It was a good suggestion, so she took it. "How do you know about the *Harvest*?"

A third alien walked into the clearing. Unlike the others, he held his empty hands up and out to his sides. She noted that this one was clean-shaven, if that was even the right word to describe it. He was the only one of the trio without a neatly trimmed beard. Huh, the beastie boys must shave after all.

They all wore similar attire, too. Though there wasn't much to their fashion choices. A simple leather kilt hung from their hips, and they'd strapped what looked like hardened animal hides to their lower legs with some kind of homespun cord or leather thong.

The third one introduced himself. "I am Risk. We met one of the other survivors from your ship—a female named Hope."

Loris felt a flash of relief to hear there were other survivors, but she didn't let her feelings show. This situation was still far too fraught with danger for her to relax.

Joy spoke up. "She made it? Where is she?"

The spokesman for the group nodded once and then explained. "We saw her this morning. Her escape pod came down much closer to our home. She was rescued by one of our brothers. We were on our way to the main crash site to assist when we saw your shuttle."

Joy seemed satisfied because she made a show of putting down her weapon and moving her hands away from the stock. Loris wasn't happy about that, but she understood this was part of Joy's personality.

She sighed and nudged the other woman with her foot. "You can't help yourself. Can you? You don't have a single distrustful bone in your body. Pick up the weapon, Joy. It could be a trick."

Joy ignored her. Instead of being sensible, the woman asked another question.

"What else can you tell us? Were there other survivors? What about the *Harvest*? Did it land safely or crash?"

Risk shifted his attention to Loris. Until then he'd been staring at Joy with an unsettling amount of interest. Male interest. The kind that made Loris tighten her grip on the rifle. There'd be none of that.

"Put down the weapon and we'll share what we know."

"You first," Loris said firmly.

The one who called himself Havoc stowed his weapons, and then both he and Risk turned to glower at their companion. He still had his sword in his hand and was giving her a cocky grin that made her want to shoot another warning shot just to make him jump.

His grin widened as if he knew what she was thinking, and she caught a glimpse of fangs behind his lips.

Fangs. Fur. Oh, and horns. She hadn't noticed the horns before, but now she couldn't stop staring at them. They swept up and back from his brow and curved around to a tapered point below his ears.

Like handles, some small, utterly mad part of her observed. *I could climb him like a tree.*

She barely registered the insane thought before the situation caught her attention again.

"For fuck's sake, Venge," Risk growled. "We talked about this."

"You talked. I wasn't listening," Vengeance said.

Joy giggled. Actually fucking giggled. Were they all losing their minds?

"You must be related. Only family bicker like that," Joy said.

Loris poked her with her toe again. "Stop laughing. We're trying to look intimidating."

"I think that ship has left orbit," Maddison said from her spot deeper inside the shuttle. Her friend managed to keep her voice steady, but there was no missing the edge to her words.

"We are clan-brothers," Havoc confirmed. Then he bared his fangs and snarled at the one they called Vengeance. "Disarm, brother. The hunt is over."

The hunt? Loris caught her breath. They'd said they were headed to the crash site to offer their assistance. Something told her these three hadn't told them the whole truth. They'd been on the hunt for something.

Her eyes narrowed. If they thought the three of them were prey to be tracked down and pounced on, they were going to be disappointed.

The cocky one held out one hand to her as he gracefully returned his blade to the scabbard on his back. "I am disarmed, little warrior. Now it's your turn."

She shot him her most intimidating glower and muttered, "Who does he think he's calling little?" Then it struck her that compared to Vengeance, she was almost petite. Okay, not really, but he was bigger than her by every metric she could think of.

He must have thought the same way because he thumped a fist to his broad chest and laughed. "You are small compared to me. Tiny, but fierce."

Loris lowered her weapon. It was time for a little trust. But only a little. "I think you just insulted me and complimented me in the same sentence. Call me Loris." She pointed down and then into the depths of the shuttle. "That's Joy, and Maddison is inside."

The three males roamed around the small camp, commenting to each other in low tones Loris couldn't quite make out. She got the sense they were assessing the situation. Risk kept looking over at the shuttle. Was he thinking about flying off with their only escape vehicle? Maybe, but it wasn't likely to happen. The ship's systems had shut down the moment they'd landed. They'd tried everything they could think of, but none of them knew how to unlock the controls, and they'd been afraid that anything they tried might lead to them damaging something important.

Eventually the three males wandered over to the campfire.

"If you want a place to sit, you'll have to find something yourselves," Joy said.

"Why are there only two spots to sit when there are three of you?" Risk asked.

"Because one of us is injured and can't move around easily," Loris explained.

To her surprise, all three looked concerned. "Is it serious? Can we do anything to help?" Havoc asked.

Vengeance looked her way, his golden eyes gleaming brightly in the light of the setting sun. "Is it you, little warrior? If it is, I will carry you to the fire and let you sit on my lap as we talk."

She stiffened. Why was he saying that crap? Was he mocking her? Or was this simply a cultural thing? Did he not realize his words could be taken as flirting? That had to be it because it had been more than a decade since anyone had dared to flirt with her, and that last time had been the result of a drunken bet.

She met his gaze and did her best to look unimpressed. Hopefully he'd get the message. "It's nothing serious, and it's not me. And I told you to stop calling me that. My name is Loris, not little warrior."

Vengeance shrugged, the simple motion making his arms and chest flex slightly. "Your name is pretty, but I like my name for you better. And even if you are not hurt, my offer to carry you stands."

Holy nukes and novas. He *was* flirting with her. She set her face into what she hoped was a stern expression, but her heart was racing as heat crept into her cheeks. The harder she tried to control it, the more flustered she got.

Damn the male to the void and back again. She wasn't interested. He was too young for her. Hell, they weren't even the same species. No. Just no.

Joy made a tiny sound that could have been a snicker, and Loris turned to glare at her. The professional matchmaker flashed her an innocent smile she didn't buy for an instant.

Well, shit.

Loris went off to find the solar-powered lanterns they'd found stashed with the rest of the emergency supplies. By the time she returned, the others were seated, and Maddison was handing out a selection of self-heating meal packs.

Soon most of them were seated by the fire while Joy stayed by the shuttle door. Risk kept glancing at Joy. Or maybe he was looking at the shuttle. She couldn't be sure.

Vengeance devoured his meal with gusto but also with surprisingly good table manners. Who *were* these males? Where were they from? Was this their home planet? She had so many questions, but they had more important matters to discuss first.

Havoc shared what he knew about the crash and the survivors. There was a lot he didn't know, but it was comforting to hear that Clarissa, Hope, and Bella had made it. All three women had been passengers on the matchmaking cruise, and while she didn't know any of them well, they'd seemed like decent sorts the few times they'd interacted.

Havoc confirmed that other members of their clan had already left for the crash site. They intended to care for any survivors and salvage what they could from the wreckage. Loris wasn't sure she liked the idea of Maddison's property being claimed by these aliens, but right now she couldn't do much about it.

The conversation had continued while she'd been distracted by thoughts of her own. They'd tossed several questions around, but the first one she fully heard was from Vengeance. His deep rumble of a voice was hard to miss.

"What made the ship crash at all?" he asked.

Loris answered him, "We had engine trouble, fell out of hyperspace, and were immediately attacked. At least, that's the impression I got when we reached the bridge."

All three males nodded.

"We were right. The scrawnies have this place well-guarded," Havoc said.

"Who are the scrawnies?" Maddison spoke for the first time.

"The verexi," Havoc clarified. "We have our own name for the scrawny bastards."

"They do that? Why?" Loris asked. She understood the verexi were territorial, but even considering their disdain for other species in general and humans in particular, they weren't normally so hostile.

Havoc nodded. "I'm certain of it. They don't want anyone coming here until they eradicate us."

"Eradicate you?" Loris had to stop herself from instinctively reaching for the weapon resting on the ground at her feet. "Why?"

Vengeance curled his top lip back to expose his fangs and then snorted. "Because we're a mistake they want to erase from existence. This is a prison planet, little warrior. We were sent here to die. We survived, and that's a problem for the scrawnies—one they want to correct."

Fuck. That was not what she wanted to hear. This would complicate any attempt to rescue them. While she considered the situation, the others kept talking.

"The verexi are still trying to kill you even though

you can't leave this place?" Joy asked with a quaver in her normally steady voice.

"They are," Risk said grimly. "And if they find out you survived, they'll kill you, too."

Oh no. No. No. No. Loris was already rising from her seat by the time Joy called out to her, "We have to shut down the beacon and the radio. Right now!"

Loris made for the shuttle. It was standard practice to activate a distress beacon. Theirs had been running since shortly after they landed, along with a recorded message that went out every hour. Both were relatively short range, but anyone in the system should be able to detect it.

The three alien males stood up together, forming a wall of muscle. "You've had a beacon going all this time?" Risk asked.

Loris ignored the question. She was already running back to the shuttle.

Joy scrambled to her feet and leaned against the nearest wall so Loris could squeeze past her and reach the cockpit.

"Ship! Deactivate distress beacon and shut down all transmissions."

"This is not a recommended course of action," the ship replied.

"Fuck recommended action. Terminate the beacon. All crew are at risk so long as that signal is active."

They'd known that sending any kind of distress call was a calculated risk, but they'd all agreed it was worth taking the chance. Both she and Joy believed they must have been taken out by an automated defense system. It was still the most likely possibility, but now they had more information.

It felt like an agonizing eternity before the ship's computer announced deactivation was complete. Loris took another twenty seconds to confirm that no signals were being broadcast and then called out to the others, "Done!"

From somewhere outside, one of the males—she thought it was Risk—asked a question so loudly she heard it inside. "Can this ship fly?"

Joy said something in reply, probably explaining that the ship had locked them out of the flight controls immediately after landing. Loris had tried the codes the captain had shouted at her as they'd left, but either she'd misheard the sequence or the captain had gotten it wrong because they didn't work.

"...will stay," one of them said. "Shuttle... too valuable." She strained to hear.

"Bring Strife and Bysshe, if he's able. If I can't access the flight systems, maybe one of them can."

Havoc spoke next. "We'll take the females to safety and be back as soon as we can."

"Take the females? Don't you dare try it. I'm not going anywhere," she muttered and settled deeper into her seat.

"I should stay too." Vengeance almost growled the words. "They will come."

"No, the females need protection."

She missed whatever was said next, but Joy's response was loud and crystal clear.

"The females would like a say in what happens next. This isn't only your decision."

"Damn right it's not!" Loris shouted.

A moment later, Joy piped up. "Loris, you've got incoming."

She was almost certain she knew who was coming inside, and she was not taking any of his shit.

Maddison cried out, her voice tight but controlled, "Don't let him hurt her!"

Damn it. Maddi didn't need this. She'd been through enough already.

Loris swore the shuttle settled to one side when Vengeance stepped inside.

"I'm not going anywhere," she said, not even bothering to turn around.

"Yes, you are, little warrior."

She expected him to threaten her or use his massive size to intimidate her into doing what he said.

She was not prepared for him to catch her by both shoulders and lift her out of the chair. "What the hell? No! Put me down!"

"Put you down. Yes. But only if you behave." He set her on her feet in a smooth motion that seemed effortless. Nukes 'n' novas, he was strong.

She caught hold of his forearm to push it away while giving him a piece of her mind, but the words turned to ash on her tongue. Heat washed through her, making her blood sizzle and her entire body ache with needs she hadn't acknowledged in years.

Instead of putting distance between them, she released his arm and set her hand in the center of the broad expanse of his chest. His fur was soft, his flesh warm, and she had to fight a sudden urge to move closer and press as much of her body as possible against his.

What was happening to her? Was she losing her mind? Doubtful, which meant it had to be something else. Something *he* was doing. Her anger rose, giving her enough of a jolt to regain some control.

She straightened her arm, using it to push herself a step back. "Stop it. Whatever weird whammy you're trying on me isn't going to work."

The look he gave her was hotter than a star. "I've done nothing."

To her shock, he reached out and gently, so gently, cupped her cheek in one callused hand. "Mine."

It took longer than she liked before she found the strength to swat his hand away. "Not yours. And not interested."

He grinned and scrunched his nose in obvious amusement. "Liar. I can smell your need, little warrior." The smug bastard licked his lips. "Delicious."

His words poured rocket fuel in the fire already blazing inside her. Her nipples tightened, and her clit swelled. Clamping her thighs together only made things worse, and within seconds her pussy was slick with proof of her desire.

"We are not having this conversation. I said no."

He growled softly, his golden gaze piercing her down to her soul. "And I said *mine*."

The word made her tremble but not out of fear. Still, she took another step back, cramming herself against the wall of the cockpit.

He caught her by one wrist and pulled with irresistible strength. She stumbled forward. He was so strong he could have broken her arm, but he managed his strength, only using enough to make her comply without injuring her in the process.

"Bully," she said.

"We don't have time for this right now. Later, you and I will play this game." Without another word, he gathered her into his arms and then slung her over one shoulder. She pummeled his back with both hands, but he ignored her. When she tried to kick, he planted one hand firmly on her upturned ass and used his other arm to restrain her legs.

There was no such thing as dignity during a fight, but Loris still felt foolish as he carried her outside. Despite the fact his shoulder dug into her stomach, and it wasn't easy to breathe while upside down, she didn't stop smacking his back or cursing in every language she knew.

They were still on the ramp when he called out to the others. "This one is mine."

This again? She filled her lungs and bellowed. "The hell I am! Put. Me. Down!"

She only quieted when Havoc moved toward Maddison, who was still seated. "I guess this means you're with me."

Maddison went pale. "What? No! I'm not with anyone. I mean, I wasn't on this cruise looking for a mate. I own the *Harvest*. That's all."

Loris struggled harder against Vengeance's hold. She was Maddison's bodyguard. No way could she let this happen. Maddison was her friend, and Joy...

Loris scanned the area quickly and spotted Joy near the campfire. When had she left the door of the shuttle? And why was she currently sitting in Risk's lap looking dazed and entirely unconcerned?

Was this whammy thing contagious?

Havoc moved over to Maddison. Loris tensed, terrified for her friend, but the big male moved with care as he crouched down in front of Maddi, his hands lifted and palms turned upward.

"You aren't safe here. None of us are. We need to leave before the scrawnies send someone to investigate."

Loris went still so she could hear better. The alien was speaking in calm, firm tones. He wanted to convince Maddi, not force her.

Apparently, Loris had wound up with the arrogant one. *Wonderful.*

"But what if it's a rescue party?" Joy asked.

She wriggled but not too much. "Put me down. Please," Loris said.

Vengeance did as she asked. Once she was on her feet, she turned to face her employer. As much as she hated this entire situation, the damned aliens weren't wrong about the danger.

"No one is coming to rescue us, Maddison. We're deep in verexi territory. I don't know how we got here or what went wrong, but we need to make the best of it."

A strong arm wrapped possessively around her waist. She turned and glared back at Vengeance. "And no, that was not me agreeing to anything. I'm simply being practical."

The smug son-of-a-beast grinned and tightened his

hold on her. "You do that. I am patient. Eventually you'll see I am right." His voice dropped to a low growl. "You *are* mine."

Risk whispered something to Joy, who flushed slightly, but her lips quirked into a brief smile.

"Joy is injured and cannot walk, so she will stay with me," Risk announced.

"But what about the verexi?" Maddison asked, still looking uncertain. "You said it wasn't safe to stay here."

"The ship is too valuable to leave behind. I will keep it and Joy safe," Risk said firmly.

Havoc spoke next, "Maddison and Loris. You have five minutes to pack food, water, and clothing. Then we must go."

Was their entire species this annoyingly bossy? Stars above, she hoped not. She caught Maddi's eye and flashed her a series of hand signals. One for reassurance. Another for caution. The last were reminders to keep at least one weapon hidden on her person at all times and to take care of herself.

It sucked harder than a black hole, but what else could they do? Staying with Joy and the shuttle would only risk more lives.

Loris hurried to the far side of the shuttle to the emergency shelter and their stash of supplies. It was time to go.

6

____

Vengeance wanted to roar in jubilation. He'd found one. A female. Well, he'd found three, but the others didn't interest him. All his attention was on his little warrior. Her hair was like moon-kissed steel, cut short at the sides and left long and curly on the top. He'd only seen hair like hers in vids. All his brothers had straight hair similar to his own. He wanted to gather her into his arms and bury his face in those silvery curls. Were they as soft as the skin of her cheek? He thought they would be.

Soon he'd find out for himself.

He had believed she was his from the first moment he'd caught her scent. It wasn't the same as his, but it was similar in the same way that Hope's matched Menace's. Even still, he had not been prepared for the raw power that erupted when they first connected. All she did was touch his arm, but in that moment, he was lost to everything but her.

Part of his mind had screamed at him to pin her against the nearest flat surface and lay claim to her body.

His cock had turned to steel and throbbed in time with his pounding heart.

Her defiance only made him want her more. The scrawnies were terrified of their creations. Bysshe had never been afraid of them, but he'd never challenged them, either. The android was controlled, deliberate, and thoughtful in all his interactions with Vengeance and his clan-brothers. He was also the closest they had ever had to a father figure.

Loris was different. She had fire in her soul, and her body was beautiful. Strong. Powerful. He'd broken more than his share of the pleasure bots the verexi had provided for their use. With Loris, he wouldn't have to worry. She was not delicate or meek in any way. She was his match in every way, even if she hadn't accepted that yet. Once they were safely away from this place, he'd show her the true meaning of pleasure. How many orgasms would it take to convince her she belonged to him? He looked forward to finding out.

When the females were ready, they all gathered near the fire. The three humans stood together, watching Vengeance and his brothers with open interest along with some trepidation. Trust would come, but not yet.

He rummaged in the bag he wore slung over one shoulder until he found what he was looking for. He handed the blaster to Risk. "You will need this more than I will."

His clan-brothers stared at the weapon. Then, with a snarl, Havoc cuffed him in the back of the head. He saw it coming and decided not to react. Now wasn't the time for them to argue.

"You took one of the weapons from the cache? That's forbidden!" Havoc said.

He laughed it off. "You think I was the only one? Nearly half the stash was missing when I got there."

"Bysshe will skin you all alive and recycle your hides to make more of those jumpsuits he likes," Havoc muttered.

"He will have to catch us first." Vengeance wanted to be gone already. Night was falling, and Loris was unfamiliar with the dangers of this place. The planet they'd crashed onto was full of threats, and a great many of them were nocturnal.

He offered Risk the weapon again. "Keep the blaster. You can use it to protect your female. Havoc and I will vanish into the woods soon. The mercenaries won't find us. They will come for you and this ship."

Risk finally took the weapon. "I will be waiting for them. They can't have it."

"The ship or the female?" Havoc asked.

"Both."

So at least one of his brothers had learned what he already knew. The three females were destined to become their mates. Loris for him, Joy for Risk, and the soft-spoken Maddison belonged to Havoc. Or she would once his brother figured it out. He wondered how long it would take. Longer than him, anyway. That was good enough for him.

"I feel the same about my little warrior. *Mine.*" He stressed the last word and added a low growl at the end to make his point clear.

Havoc scrubbed a hand through his beard and looked

thoughtful. "I don't know if Maddison is mine...but she needs my protection. She is too gentle for this world. And for me."

Vengeance nodded. Hope had a quiet strength to her, but Maddison was wary, her eyes shadowed with remembered pain. He'd seen it before. All the fa'rel had endured torture and experimentation at the hands of their captors. They rarely spoke of it, but they didn't need to. They all bore scars on their bodies and on their psyches.

It was time to go. He and his brothers locked eyes and nodded once. They bowed their heads and knocked horns in a ritual they'd created for themselves.

"Good hunting, my brothers."

Vengeance took Loris by the hand and led her into the trees. Havoc gestured for Maddison to follow him and went a different way. The two women looked uncertain, and Loris made a low sound of protest. "We're not traveling together?"

"No. Separate is safer. Four of us traveling together would make it difficult to mask our trail."

"You don't understand. Maddison is my..." Loris sighed. "She pays me to protect her. I should stay with her."

He shook his head. "Havoc is her protector now. And I am yours."

His little warrior looked entirely unimpressed at this announcement. "I can take care of myself."

"Anywhere else, I would agree with you, but not here. This is my home. You need to trust me to keep you safe."

Even in the fading light, he saw the way her eyes crinkled and her lips twitched into a brief grin. "The local wildlife isn't the only thing I'm worried about, big guy. As it happens, you're at the top of my potential threat list."

He tightened his grip on her hand, reveling in how well it fit inside his larger one. "I'm the most dangerous thing in these woods, but I'm not interested in hurting you." He turned to stare down at her, his grin wide enough she could see his fangs. "The only screams you'll make tonight are ones of pleasure."

"There will be no screaming of any kind unless you piss me off. If that happens, I can't guarantee you won't be making all sorts of unhappy noises."

She was magnificent like this, her words lashing out like knives in the dark and her warrior spirit on full display.

"Why do you deny it? I know you feel the same things I do." He drew in a long breath. "I smell your need, little one. You are a feast for my senses. I want to know it all. The feel of your bare skin, the taste of your mouth, the heat of your—"

"Whoa! I haven't agreed to anything apart from going with you so we can do our best to stay alive. I'm not thrilled about anything that's happened since the ship went down. No matter what you think you smell, I am not in the mood!"

She slowed for a moment to look up at him. "I don't understand any of this. Why the hell would you want me? Do you hit on every female you come across? I mean, you're young, hot as hell, and quite literally horny..." She gestured to his horns. "But does this approach actually work for you?"

It was all he could do not to stop and demand she explain herself. He wasn't hitting her. He'd never do that. Confused and distracted by her comments, he led her through the trees. They moved slowly, careful not to leave more traces of their passage than necessary.

The last traces of daylight faded away within minutes, leaving them to navigate in the dark. No moon brightened the sky for now, but the starlight was enough to let him find their way.

At first, Loris kept up with him, but once it went completely dark, her pace fell off. "How the fuck can you see anything? It's as dark as a black hole at midnight out here."

"The scrawnies created us to fight the wars they couldn't. They designed us to have every advantage possible over their enemies. Night vision, higher pain tolerance, strength, endurance, even faster healing."

Loris stumbled and bumped into him. "They *made* you?" she asked.

"They did. I was raised in a lab and tested on more times than there are stars in the sky."

He waited, unsure what her reaction would be. It wasn't what he expected. She leaned into him, close enough strands of her hair caressed his arm. "That must have been hard. I'm sorry, Vengeance."

"You have nothing to apologize for. The verexi experimented on me. On us. None of the other species were involved." He thought for a moment and then added, "The scrawnies kept us a secret."

"Saying I'm sorry is an expression. A way to offer sympathy. As for the scrawnies, I can understand why those brittle bundles of sticks wanted to create super soldiers, but I can't believe they actually *did* it."

"That's why we're here. On this planet. The experiment didn't work, and they wanted to get rid of the evidence." He slapped his chest. "That meant killing all of us. Only we didn't let that happen."

"How many of you are there?" she asked, her voice gentler than he'd ever heard her before.

"Nine now. Some died long ago. Ravage died when our ship crashed. Shatter was killed by a venomous creature that lives in the water. My clan-brother Rage was killed trying to escape. We think that was when they decided to get rid of us."

"Interesting names you have. I don't suppose one of you is called Rainbow or Snuggles or something like that."

He scoffed at the mere idea. "We named ourselves. Do you imagine any of my brothers would choose such a name?"

"What about your sisters?"

"The scrawnies never created any females."

Loris made a disgusted sound. "Of course they didn't. They probably thought males would make better fighters."

"They might have. Or they might not have considered it. They have no gender." He shuddered slightly. "They threatened to castrate us if we continued to defy orders. I think they might have done it, but Bysshe reminded them that they wanted soldiers, so making us less aggressive wasn't a good idea."

"Wait. There are no females on this planet? None at all? And you came here straight from the verexi lab?"

"You are the first female I have ever touched, little warrior." He gave in to his desire and drew her into his arms. "I like this."

To his amusement, she bumped her hip against the hard ridge of his cock. "I can tell. But now I think I understand why you're interested. You've never been near a woman before. You're young, randy, and gods...are you a virgin?"

He didn't want to stay here long. They had to get further from the shuttle before they set up camp for the night, but he needed to clear up something first.

"I've had sex. Many, many times. Only with pleasure bots, but some of them had instructional programs. I rated very highly on their assessment tests."

"I just bet you did," she whispered.

Her words broke his mind. He forgot about the need to get clear of the shuttle. He moved his hand to the back of her head, holding her still as he leaned over to kiss her. He had to know what she tasted like.

He brushed his mouth over hers, feeling the silken warmth of her lips. She started to stiffen in his arms. He knew she was about to tell him to stop, so he cut off her words with a kiss.

Perfection. Soft. Silky. Warm. He ran his tongue across the seam of her lips, and she parted them for him with a moan that vibrated across his tongue and all the way to his cock.

Their tongues tangled, her fingers curving into his biceps as she rose on her toes to kiss him back. This was so much better than he'd imagined. Every second was new and unpredictable. Her surrender was glorious, and the scent of her arousal was the sweetest scent in all the worlds.

"Mine," he growled against her mouth.

She laughed and nipped his lip. "No. This is merely a moment of temporary insanity. That's all. Enjoy it while it lasts."

She still didn't understand. This wasn't temporary. It was forever. He would never let her go. Did she think she could walk away now? Or choose another of his brothers? *Never.* He'd kill anyone who touched her.

"You will stay with me. Always. You are my female. The one I will cherish, protect, and pleasure in any way you desire."

The kiss ended when she shook her head. "I'm old, Vengeance. Too old for you. No man has ever been really interested in me, even when I was young." She laughed softly. "And that was a long time ago. I'm not what you want. You just don't know it yet."

He snarled, caught her by the waist, and kissed her until she stopped trying to escape his hold.

"I know what I want." He grabbed one of her hands and drew it down between his legs, letting her feel how hard he was. "You are my female, Loris. I will never stop wanting you. That is how it is with Menace and my brothers. They have claimed the other females. I saw Hope. She looked at my brother with affection. She touched him without fear. She proclaimed him as her mate to all within hearing. This is how it will be."

"You don't know what you're saying. You don't know a thing about me."

Her voice was softer now, filled with the first whispers of doubt. He kissed her again. "I know enough. I was certain the moment I caught your scent. You were meant for me." He nuzzled her cheek.

Again she laughed, but she rested her hands on his shoulders, her fingers caressing him in small circles that made him crave more. Would it be wrong to take her now? To lift her so she could wrap her legs around his waist as he drove himself into her body? Fuck, he wanted to, but there was a reason he couldn't. What was it? He had to fight through the lust that fogged his mind to remember. The enemy. Yes. Someone would come to investigate. They had to go.

"Soon," he promised her as he kissed her again. "We'll do this again soon, but we must go. The moons will rise in an hour or so, but we can't wait. Walk behind me with your hands on my back. I will guide you."

"I can do that. You can be my own personal seeing-eye-sex-god."

"There's a god of sex?" he asked as she moved into place behind him.

"I only meant you're very attractive."

He chuckled. "I will be your sex god. You'll see."

Loris didn't answer, but she didn't have to. They both knew he spoke the truth.

7

―――――

Loris followed behind Vengeance and did her best to keep up. The small part of her mind not busy on keeping her footing as they marched through the night-soaked woods ran through a litany of questions she couldn't answer.

What in the nine hells was she doing?

Would Maddison be okay?

Was Vengeance insane, or did he really intend to claim her as his female?

Round and round she went, her mind whirling while her body kept reacting to Venge's in ways that made her blush.

More than once her hands slid from the soft fur of his back to the band that held his kilt in place. What would he look like naked? Did he have fur *everywhere*? He seemed confident that whatever his equipment was, they were biologically compatible. However, given the size of the rest of him, she had concerns. She couldn't seem to hold on to them for very long, though. The more time she spent with him, the harder it was to think about anything else. Even her worries about Maddi faded. The only thought that lingered was how Vengeance made her feel. He was maddeningly stubborn, but his desire for her was obvious. He *wanted* her, and he wasn't being subtle about it.

Hells, he probably didn't know the meaning of the word. Everything about him was brash, bold, and far sexier than he had any right to be. Damn him.

An hour ago, she hadn't known he existed. Now he was all she could think about. When they stopped for the night, would he really do what he'd said? She knew the answer to that. Of course he would. The real question was, would she let him? She laughed at herself. She was too far gone to stop now.

If this was her last night of living, why not enjoy herself? Death might come for her either way. A few seconds of pleasure wouldn't change that.

The moons rose eventually, and they provided enough light for her to make her own way. They descended steadily. Vengeance moved like a phantom, barely making a sound. She did her best, but it had been far too long since she'd done something like this. She was out of practice and out of shape compared to the soldier she'd once been.

After what might have been an hour, they took a break. She unclipped a water bottle from her bag and drank from it. As tempted as she was to lean against a nearby tree, she stayed standing. She had no idea what might be lurking in the branches. Hells, for all she knew the tree's sap was poisonous or acid or something equally deadly.

"You move well," Vengeance said. "What military did you fight for?"

She smiled at the directness of the query. He really didn't have much in the way of filters. "Humans don't have a military. It's not permitted. But we have mercenary forces that do more or less the same thing. We did whatever we were paid to do. Mostly planetary defense, but we took other jobs, too. Eliminating raiders. Reacquiring lost assets. The usual things."

"Ah. I didn't know that." He took a drink from his waterskin, the leather and simple stopper so different from her own plas-steel container.

"But you are not a mercenary anymore. You said you protect Maddison."

"I was hired as her bodyguard ten years or so ago. It's a prestige thing for the rich and powerful. Most of the time it was easy work." That was true enough. The only person who posed a real threat to Maddi's safety was her bastard husband. When he summoned his wife, Loris was never allowed to accompany her. She'd wait nearby and do what she could to help her friend in the aftermath.

"Havoc won't let anything happen to her. Will he? He won't hurt her? She's been through a lot. Her former husband was a mean bastard."

"If her male abused her, why didn't she leave?" He moved close enough she could see his face now.

"She couldn't. Their marriage contract was written so only he could break it, and he liked having her under his control. Once the contract expired, she left, and I went with her.

"So she was a prisoner?"

"She was. A bird caught in a golden cage. Wealth, luxury, everything she could ask for, but she couldn't leave. Not even when..." Loris didn't finish the statement.

"Havoc will take care of her. The fa'rel understand too well what it's like to live in captivity."

His reassurances helped. "Good. If he does anything to her, though, I will gut him and leave him to whatever scavengers live on this planet."

"You won't have to do that. If he harms your friend, I will beat him for you."

"I fight my own battles, thank you."

"Not anymore." He thumped his chest. "I have sworn to protect you."

Arguing with him was a waste of breath, and now wasn't the time to explain the concept of consent. She changed the subject.

"You mentioned the fa'rel. Is that what you call yourselves?"

"It's what the scrawnies called us."

"And you kept the name?"

"Only that one. We chose our own names when we were still young. I am Vengeance because one day I will take revenge on the scrawnies for what they did to us." He grinned. "And I didn't like being called Research Subject Nine."

"I bet you didn't."

She offered up more information about herself in exchange. "I kind of named myself, too. Loris was the name of a character in a story I read when I was growing up. My parents had lifetime contracts with an asteroid mining consortium. They were only supposed to have two kids who would take over their contracts when they got too old to work. I was their third child."

"They hid my existence for a few years and then sold me to another family. I don't remember them or the name they gave me. I was sold or passed along to several other families after that. Sometimes I was given a new name. Sometimes they didn't bother and called me by the last one I'd been given."

"They passed you from family to family like a possession?" The last word Vengeance spoke came out as more of a growl.

"Technically, I was a possession. Bought and sold based on what care I needed versus my value as a future worker."

"You mean slave." It wasn't a question.

"They had prettier words for it, but yes." She had a flash of pride as she remembered the day she'd found a way to escape. "But I wasn't under contract yet. I was an investment of sorts. Only by then, no one thought I'd be worth much. Too stubborn." She grinned.

He laughed, and the sound rolled through the night. It made her feel good.

"Anyway, I ended up getting sold to a mercenary group. They trained me and gave me a job I actually liked. I stayed with them until my contract ended more than twenty years later."

She spread out her hands and took a small bow. "And that's my story."

"Thank you for sharing it. I want to know all your stories, Loris. But for now, we need to get moving." He pointed ahead. "We'll be back in the forest in another hour. Then we can stop for the night."

"What do you mean, back in the forest?" She gestured around them. "Isn't this a fucking forest?"

"These are just trees and bushes. The true forest is below us. You'll see."

He put away his water skin and set off again. She followed after him, still wondering what the difference was. A bunch of trees were a forest. That's how it was. Maybe it was a translation error.

The difference became clear even about forty minutes later. The canopy overhead blocked all but a few stray beams of moonlight. Trees grew so thickly their roots were tangled in large knots, some of them wrapped around moss-covered boulders.

She could barely see anything unless it was right next to her, so she fell in behind Vengeance and let him guide her.

"So, this is what you meant by the true forest?"

"It is. Though this is only the beginning. It gets thicker farther in. We won't be going that way. It would take too long."

"Which way are we going?" Not that the information would do her any good. She had no idea where they were or where they were headed.

"For now, we'll stop. Tomorrow I'll work out the

fastest route home. We need to reach the river, but I've never been this way before."

"What! Never? So we're lost?" she asked.

"We're not lost. I used the stars to navigate until we lost sight of them. Now we will stop until daylight so I can find some landmarks. This is how we live, little warrior. We have no maps, no compasses, or satellites to show us where we are."

Right. As advanced as the fa'rel were, they'd crashed on this world and lacked most of the technology and equipment she took for granted. "If we're not lost, can you tell me how long it will take us to get to your home?"

He thought about that for a few seconds before answering. "If things go well, we'll arrive tomorrow evening. If things are difficult, we'll spend another night out in the wilds. I'd rather not do that."

"Me either." She glanced around, but nothing in her limited range of vision looked promising in terms of shelter. "Where are we hunkering down? I've got a thermal blanket in my bag, but I don't see much dead wood we could use to build a lean-to. Is it safe to rack out under one of these big roots?"

"Stop trying to break my translator," he grumbled good-naturedly. "And to answer your question, it's not wise to sleep on the ground. Something would try to eat us, and the moss holds water like a sponge."

He pressed his hand down on a patch of the stuff and it squelched loudly.

"Lovely. So, what's your plan?"

He patted the bag resting on his hip. "We go up."

"Up. Sure. Right. Obviously." She stared into the gloom overhead. "I'm going to need more details."

"Trust me, little warrior. I do this every time I hunt." He pulled something from the bag and shook it between his hands.

While he did that, she rummaged around in her own pack and found a small light-cube. "Can we risk a little light? I'd really like to see what you're doing."

"Some. Light would be helpful for this next part."

She made a quick adjustment to the cube's settings and then activated it with a double tap to one side. An aura of amber light appeared and slowly expanded until she could see a few meters in all directions.

Vengeance held something that looked like some kind of netting in one hand and a coil of slender rope slung over his other shoulder. His bag was on the ground at his feet, and while she watched, he tucked several lengths of cord into a thong of leather tied around his biceps.

"What are you doing?" she asked.

He flicked one finger skyward. "Making us a bed. Stay in the light and don't try to follow me up."

"Like that's going to happen," she muttered as he bounded to the nearest tree and leaped for one of the lower branches. He moved so fast she could barely follow him with her eyes, never mind the rest of her.

The first time he jumped from one tree to another, she almost screamed in surprise. The next time he did it, she had figured out what he was doing. The net was now suspended between several trees. It created a sort of platform high enough above the ground to be safe from predators. At least, she assumed none of the local carnivores were large enough to reach that high.

"If you fall, I am not kissing your boo-boos better." She had no idea why she'd said anything about kissing him, but the words were out before her brain caught up to her mouth.

"Again with the nonsensical words. You're welcome to kiss any part of me you like." He finished securing the last corner of the net and hopped off the branch and into the center of the makeshift sleeping platform he'd made.

This time, she did scream a little. She was certain the delicate netting would break beneath the load, and he'd plummet to the ground.

It dipped a little, but that was all.

He grinned down at her. "And for future reference, I do not fall. My reflexes are too good for that."

She ignored his boast. Mostly because she suspected he was right. The verexi might have missed the mark when it came to the personality of their experiments, but Vengeance and the others were as close to physical perfection as she'd ever seen or heard about.

Instead of climbing down one of the trees, Vengeance bent over, grabbed the edge of the net in both hands, and somersaulted into open air. He seemed to unfold as he fell, his grip releasing as he straightened to land feet first on the ground beside her.

"Show-off."

He turned to look down at her, grinning from ear to ear. "Tell me you were not impressed, and I will call you a liar."

"Oh, it was impressive. Also, risky and unnecessary."

She nudged his bag with the toe of her shoe. "I see how you intend to get in and out of our mid-air mattress. My question is. How in the hells do you think I'm getting my ass up there?"

"Easy. I will carry you."

"Nope. No way. You're not lugging me up into the trees like I'm cargo."

The look he gave her made her brain turn to mush. "Say no to me again, little warrior. *Please.*"

She raised her chin and met his gaze. "No."

He moved faster than she thought possible. One second he stood across from her, and the next he was behind her with one arm across her waist and the other cupping her breast through her shirt. "Now we play."

She froze, her heart slamming against her ribs as he lowered his head and traced a path of open-mouthed kisses along the side of her neck. "You will do as I say."

"No, I won't." She didn't even pretend it wasn't a lie, but this was the game he wanted to play, and she was all in.

"Then I will have to show you what happens when you defy me." The arm around her waist moved until one large hand covered her mons, his fingers pressed along the seam of her pussy. "You don't get to come until you do what you're told."

She bit back a moan as sparks of desire flowed over her skin. This was happening. She wanted it to happen, but she couldn't give in to him. Not yet. Not until she knew what he wanted from her. Once he made his demand, something told her it wouldn't be long before she gave in.

8

____

He'd never been this close to losing control. It took everything he had not to tear off her clothes, bend her over a stone, and fuck her until her screams of pleasure filled the surrounding woods.

That would happen, but not yet. He wanted her to sass him, to challenge him. He liked her fire. It made him burn but without the anger that always came when he spent too much time with his clansmen. His brothers annoyed him. Loris did not.

She seemed to understand what he wanted, or maybe she wanted the same thing. She wriggled in his grip, her ass grinding against his cock as she attempted to break free of him. Not that she could. He was too strong, and she... he smiled to himself. His little warrior wasn't trying that hard.

"You keep talking about obedience, but so far you haven't given me any orders. You can't punish me for something I haven't done yet."

"You argued when I told you I'd carry you to bed. That counts."

She chuckled, a low, throaty sound that made his cock twitch. "Oh, sweet boy, if you think that was an argument, you are in for a surprise."

"I. Am. No. Boy." He growled each word, pressing against her sex with each syllable. "Insults are also grounds for punishment."

"This game has a lot of rules. Maybe you should tell me what you want."

He nipped the soft flesh along her throat before answering. "I want you to admit that you belong to me. That you are *mine*."

"Nope. Not yours."

"You are. And now I will prove it to you."

Letting go of her wasn't easy, but it had to be done. He kept one hand on her hip as he turned and spilled the contents of his bag on the moss-covered ground. He spotted his blanket and snagged it with his claws. It was warm, soft, and waterproof, which made it perfect for what he had in mind. He tossed it down on a nearby rock and managed to get it spread out enough to create a dry, comfortable spot for Loris.

"What are you doing? I thought you said we were sleeping up there?"

"No one is sleeping yet."

"Oh. Right. So..."

He pointed to her and then to the blanket. "You may undress yourself, or I will do it for you. Then you get on that rock."

She locked her arms across her chest and glared at him. "Try again."

He snarled. "Naked. Now."

"You want me naked? You do it."

That's exactly what he'd wanted her to say. "It would be my pleasure."

"You tricked me!" Her voice lilted with the barest hint of laughter.

"I don't know what you're talking about, stubborn female. Now hold still. I don't want to tear your clothes. I do not believe you have many others."

She relaxed her stance but held her ground, letting him do all the work. He took his time, forcing himself to go slowly and enjoy this moment. The long-sleeved top she wore was easy to unfasten, each undone clasp showing more of her golden skin. He slipped it off her shoulders and down her arms, placing it carefully on the blanket. Beneath the shirt she wore a pale pink contraption that held her breasts in place. He'd seen this in the vids the scrawnies let them watch. Some females used them to change their body shape. He didn't understand why, and he didn't like the way the straps dug into her shoulders.

He extended his claws and sliced through the fabric, pulling it away from her skin to avoid injury.

"Hey! I thought you said you didn't want to tear my stuff!"

"This is unnecessary and looks painful."

As the fabric fell away, her breasts came into view, heavy globes of soft flesh with nipples already tight with desire. Overcome, he gathered them in his hands and buried his face in them. Turning his head, he captured one nipple with his mouth and sucked on it.

A moan of pleasure told him he'd done it right. Another suck and then a gentle nip as he played with her other breast with his fingers. He had to take care not to let his claws prick her.

She set her hands on his shoulders, her fingers stroking his fur as she moaned and arched her body closer to his mouth.

When he pleasured her, she stopped arguing. This was important information, which he filed away for future consideration.

He didn't stop what he was doing, but he did let go with one hand to continue undressing her. It was more difficult to undo her pants without looking at what he was doing, but he managed. Once that was done, he had enough room to slide his hand down her belly and over the mound of her sex. She bucked against his hand, her breath coming faster now.

She was ready. He moved fast, tugging down her pants and pulling her legs and feet free. Shoes were a problem, but he wrested them off her feet. He was in a hurry now, so he gathered up all her cast-off clothing and tossed it onto the blanket. Now, it was her turn.

She laughed as he walked her backward, his hands on the full curve of her hips. The scent of her drove him mad with need. He wanted to spread her out and explore every part of her body. But that would have to wait until he had her somewhere safe. Home, probably. Then he'd keep her in bed for days. Maybe weeks.

He lifted her onto the seat he'd made for her and then

stood back to drink in her beauty for the first time. She looked at him with a mix of vulnerability and defiance.

Her curves were beautiful, lush and full. Parts of her body were marked with subtle stripes, especially across her breasts, belly, and chest. He traced his fingers over some of them. Curious. "Battle scars?" he finally asked.

"Nothing so glorious. Just signs of aging. Skin stretches. Things sag," she said with a shrug.

"You *are* glorious. All of you. Softness over strength. I like it." He inhaled deeply. "I think it's time I learned one of your secrets, little warrior."

"What secret?"

"How you taste."

She groaned and let her head fall back. "You really are too good to be true. I mean, apart from the cockiness."

"I'm not cocky. I'm that good." He moved between her legs, letting his hands run up the lush flesh of her thighs. The sight made him burn like a star, and he let himself fall into her heat.

His senses swam. Sweetness on his tongue, the sounds of her moans guiding his moves as he learned what she liked best. Gentle licks made her quiver while hard flicks of his tongue caused her to swear and rock her hips against his mouth.

She gripped his horns, using them to pull him in close. "Yes. That. Just like that. Fuck. That's so good. Venge...yes!"

The sound of his name on her tongue made him wild. A sound vibrated up from his chest, a low rumbling noise he'd only made a few times before. The vibrations it caused made Loris cry out again.

He'd imagined this a thousand times. Pleasure with a willing, living female—one who wanted him as much as he wanted her.

"Harder, Venge. Use your fingers. Fuck me with them. You said you'd make me come."

He did as she asked but never gave her enough to find her release. He held her on the brink, making her shake and moan until she gasped in need.

"Please. I want... I need..."

He raised his head to meet her eyes. "Say it."

Her eyes widened. "Now?"

"If you want to come, yes. I want to hear you say it. Tell me who you belong to."

She muttered something under her breath. He was pretty sure it was a curse.

"I belong to you, Vengeance. You're a cocky, sexy, son of a bitch, and apparently, I'm yours." She waggled her brows at him. "Now make with the orgasm already."

She'd said it. She'd accepted his claim. *Mine.*

He slid another finger into her channel and then latched on to the throbbing pearl of her clitoris with his mouth. He sucked and lashed at the tender nub, driving her into a frenzy of passion that made her moan and quiver.

He took her to the brink again, but this time he drove her over the edge. Her inner walls flexed around his fingers as she gasped his name. He didn't stop. She needed more time and attention before her body would be able to accommodate him. He was too big to rush this moment, so he forced himself to take his time and ply his new mate with as much pleasure as she could take.

When she was truly ready, he straightened up, wiped his mouth with the back of one hand, and then leaned down to kiss her. "Say it again."

"Already?"

"For me." He didn't want to play the game right now. They'd have more time for that later.

She smiled softly, her brown eyes full of warmth and something else... something he hadn't expected. Trust. "I belong to you, Vengeance. And that means you belong to me."

"Yes. I do."

He moved between her legs again, taking hold of her hips to slide her into position. A quick tug at the knot holding his kilt in place, and he was naked, his cock rising up between his thighs. He gripped it with one hand, pumping himself with hard, sharp strokes before guiding himself to her slick opening. Looking down at her body laid out like a decadent feast, he knew he was the luckiest male in the galaxy.

9

———

STILL BREATHLESS AND quivering from the force of her orgasm, Loris didn't have the brain capacity to think about her answer. She spoke from the heart and discovered something she hadn't known about herself. She was lonely. She wanted him. Not just physically, though her attraction to him was off the charts levels of crazy. She wanted a partner. Someone to tease and argue with, who called her on her shit. Even Maddi, dear friend though she was, didn't have the right personality to push back at her.

Vengeance did.

He'd given her more pleasure in one session than she'd known in a lifetime. Now it was his turn. But he didn't drive into her the way she expected him to. He entered her slowly, drawing out the moment and giving her body time to adjust.

Fuck, it felt good. He was thick enough that his cock pressed tightly against her channel, lighting up long-forgotten nerves every centimeter of the way. He was halfway in when he paused and stroked a finger over her aching clit. "I'm not hurting you?"

That simple question broke something deep inside her. No one had ever asked her that in any context. They hadn't cared enough to consider her feelings.

No one but him.

"This is the opposite of pain. I want more, Venge."

He rocked his hips and slid deeper still. This time, she felt something new. As he moved, she realized what it was. What *they* were. Ridges. Her toes curled as he pushed into her, pleasure piling on top of pleasure.

"Yes!"

She lifted her legs, wrapping them around his hips, her heels digging into his back as she tried to make him move.

He laughed at her attempts. "And you call me the bossy one." He withdrew and then drove himself deep again. "I am in charge right now, little warrior. Lie back and let me show you how it will be between us."

She relented, but she couldn't help tossing one more barb as she did as he instructed. "For now, you're in charge. Next time, I am."

"We'll see."

After that, her brain shorted out, and she lost the ability to speak. He took her hard, fangs flashing in the amber light, his golden fur streaked with shadows. His claws came out enough to sting where they sank into her hips. She didn't mind. The touch of pain only amplified the pleasure she experienced.

She gripped his wrists to steady herself against his thrusts. The rock beneath her was probably leaving bruises, but she didn't care. All she wanted was more. More of his cock. More of his kisses. More of *him*.

Their eyes met, a hundred thoughts and feelings conveyed between them without either of them saying a word.

He drove himself balls deep inside her. Instead of withdrawing, he bent over her and broke her grip so he could wrap one arm around her shoulders. His kisses scorched her lips, the hunger in his eyes burning like twin suns.

She didn't answer him with words. Instead, she tangled her hand in the silken mane of his hair and kissed him back.

They rocked together, his thick cock hitting all the right places. He groaned. She shuddered, and together they danced their way to the edge of ecstasy before letting themselves tumble over it.

His roar tore through the night air, a primal sound that should have terrified her. It didn't. This massive, dangerous male was no threat to her. Though if he had really been created with high endurance, she was in serious trouble.

She wasn't sure what would happen now. Would they talk? Snuggle? Or would he carry her up to their bed, roll over, and go to sleep?

It turned out the answer was none of the above. Instead of pulling out, his cock thickened, the ridges she'd sensed pulsing as they pushed against her inner walls.

She flexed, and he groaned, his eyes boring into hers. "Don't move. We are locked this way. If you..."

She rocked her hips and flexed her inner walls,

squeezing his cock. He shuddered, his eyes rolling up as she erupted into an unexpected orgasm.

A single thought passed through her head as she lost herself to pleasure. She was right. Vengeance really was a sex god.

She barely noticed the odd tingling at first. Her wrists felt strange, like tiny sparks were zipping across her skin.

"The hell?" she said.

"Mmm?" Vengeance sounded almost as out of it as she felt. Then he stiffened, one hand slamming into his chest. "What?"

"Good question." She raised one arm and stared at her wrist suspiciously. *Please don't be bugs. Please don't be bugs.*

Nope. No bugs. In fact, she couldn't see anything. Not at first.

Then faint lines appeared on her skin, darkening until she looked like she'd been painted... or tattooed. Lines encircled her wrist on either side, crossing over in the middle.

"I have no idea what this is. Do you?" She gestured to her arm.

Vengeance wasn't looking at her. He'd carefully eased himself upward and now stared down at his chest.

Large, dark lines ran crossed from his shoulders to his flanks, each of them intersecting in the center of his chest. They were the same markings, but in a different place.

When he looked up at last, his expression was one of pure joy. "I knew it. You are mine. You see? These are the same marks the others have."

She narrowed her gaze. "You never mentioned that before. Hope has these marks? They all do?"

"I saw these markings on Hope and Menace. Bysshe mentioned the others had them, too. He threw back his head and laughed. The vibration traveled through his body and into hers, reminding her that they were still locked together.

She glanced at her wrists again. "I always did want to get tattoos, but I never found a design I liked enough to wear forever. I guess these will do." She ran her finger along the lines that marked his chest. "Especially since they're a matched set."

They spent more time locked together, admiring the new markings and enjoying the intimacy of the moment. After that, they cleaned up, saw to a few bodily needs, and got ready for bed. In the end, she did let him carry her up on his back. Which led to another round of sex, laughter, and orgasms.

If she died tomorrow, she'd leave this plane with no regrets and more than a few aching muscles. She didn't regret those, either.

10

———

Dawn was his favorite time of day. Everything was new again, and the rising sun meant he'd made it through another night. That wasn't something he took for granted. Not after the life he'd led. Waking up free was the best feeling he'd known. Until now. Waking up free *and* with Loris curled up beside him was even better.

Most nights he was away from home he used the mesh as a hammock instead of a sleeping platform, but that wouldn't have been comfortable with two of them sharing the space. Sex would have been more challenging, too. Though they had discovered the platform had its own issues. He'd nearly thrown Loris off when his orgasm made him buck hard while she was on top. She'd made him promise to refrain from any more platform sex until he made her a safety harness. He'd grudgingly agreed but only because they needed to get some rest.

Loris was an early riser, too. So by the time the sun was up, they were packed and ready to go. The last thing he needed to do was to check their location, and that meant another round of tree climbing.

This time he needed to go all the way to the top of the canopy, which meant leaving Loris on her own.

"Venge, I'll be fine. I'll sit on my favorite rock with my rifle in my lap. If anything moves, I'll shoot it." She winked at him. "So announce yourself before you drop out of the trees."

It still didn't feel right. He was her protector, but he didn't have another option. At least she had the rifle.

It took him a few minutes to reach a spot he could see above the canopy. He had to go farther than he wanted to from Loris's position, but he eventually found a tree that worked.

With one ear cocked to listen for Loris, he used the rest of his senses to gather information. The rising sun was his best indication of direction, but he found a few landmarks he recognized. Home was on the far side of a distant set of hills. He could see the spot where the river had carved a path on its way through. Once they reached the river, it would be an easy trek back. The challenge would be getting there.

He'd opted to take a different route back, so Havoc could return the same way they'd come. Maddison wasn't as hardy as Loris and would be challenged even by the easier route. Neither of them had mentioned their plans to anyone else, but Vengeance knew his brother. He'd want to make things easier for Maddison if he could.

He worried about Risk the most. It was only a matter of time before someone came to check out the beacon the shuttle had broadcast since landing. It might take them longer to track it down now that it was turned off, but it wouldn't stop them. The verexi had sent more than a dozen mercenaries and for-hire kill teams after the fa'rel already. Now with more potential witnesses on the planet, they'd send more.

As if his thoughts had summoned them, a small vessel appeared over the horizon. It flew low, which told him they were likely using scanners to search for something. Probably the shuttle. *Shit.*

He took a final look around, trying to memorize the route they needed to take. Then he dropped back under the cover of the tree canopy and hurried back to where he'd left Loris.

Halfway down, he smelled the acrid tang of a recently fired energy weapon and accelerated his descent to little more than a controlled series of falls from branch to branch.

Once he caught sight of her, he calmed slightly. She was alone and looked unhurt and relatively unconcerned. She stood on top of the same rock she'd been sitting on when he last saw her with her pulse rifle aimed at something a short distance beyond a tangle of roots.

"What happened?" he demanded.

"Something moved, so I shot it." She indicated the direction she'd been aiming. "No idea what it was, but I don't know if it was alone."

She glanced his direction. "Did you find us a way home?"

"I did." He didn't mention the ship he'd seen. The only thing they could do right now was to put as much distance as possible between them and the shuttle.

He thought about Risk and felt a pang of regret that he couldn't be there to help. *Good hunting, my brother.*

He dropped the last few meters to the forest floor. With his blade in hand, he stalked over to where she'd indicated. A dead black fang lay on its side. Half of its head was gone, and the open wound steamed slightly in the cool morning air.

"It's dead. Come over and see what you killed. Nice shot, by the way."

"Was it dangerous? Or did I kill this planet's version of Bambi?" she asked.

He had no idea what a Bambi was, but he assumed they weren't an aggressive species. "It's a black fang, and it would have happily eaten you for breakfast."

She joined him by the body. "Ugly beasties. Aren't they? Is this as big as they get?"

It was a young adult, only about a meter and a half long. "This one isn't fully grown. They get about half again as big."

She poked the partially destroyed head with her foot. "I see why you call them that. Their teeth are as black as the rest of them."

"We keep the names simple. Easier to remember that way. Black fang. Tusk-hoppers. Blue death."

She frowned. "Blue death? What in the nine hells is that?"

"An aquatic creature." He held up one hand and balled it into a fist. "About this big. Bright blue. Squishy shape, and very poisonous. Do *not* touch. That is how Shatter died.

"Got it. No poking the blue squishy things. I'm sorry

about your brother, Venge. I hope wherever his spirit is, there's good hunting."

He looked at her in surprise. "You think there is something for us after we die? Even though we are unnatural things?"

She didn't hesitate. "I do. I don't think you're unnatural, either. The verexi might have assembled the pieces differently, but the building blocks must be the same as everyone else's."

He'd never thought about it that way. It made a comforting sort of sense.

He smiled and touched her cheek with his fingertips. "Thank you."

To his delight, she reached up to cover his hand with hers. "You're welcome. Now, is there anything else I should know about things that might want to kill me?"

"I'll tell you more about the local wildlife while we walk. Are you ready?"

"Lead the way."

Six hours of hard walking later, they discovered a problem. Instead of a gentle descent to the river, the heavy tree cover had hidden a plateau that ended in a steep drop to the river valley.

"Well, fuck. That's inconvenient," Loris said. "Though the view is spectacular. I've never been to a planet this lush or this orange. Something about the spectrum of the sunlight, maybe?"

"Bysshe said the sunlight here is brighter than

standard for life-producing planets. I wouldn't know, because this is the only world I've ever seen. The scrawnies kept us on a barren moon. No plants or animals, and not much of an atmosphere. They generated enough atmo to keep everyone on the base alive, but nowhere else."

"For the record? I was not a fan of the verexi before we met. Now? I really don't like them. If we ever get off this planet, we're going to kick their asses for what they did to you and your brothers. Not to mention what they did to the *Harvest* and everyone on board."

We. He liked it. She was already thinking of herself as part of his life. He moved to kiss her but froze before his mouth met hers.

A strange noise came from somewhere to their left. Two short, booming beats followed by one long one. He had no idea what had made that sound, but it couldn't be anything good.

"What was *that?*"

"I don't know, and I don't want to find out. We need to leave."

"Excellent idea." She raised one eyebrow and swept one hand out to indicate the cliff. "Any suggestions on how we do that? And do not say you'll carry me."

"No." He patted the bag at his hip. "This time, I'm going to tie you up."

She eyed him warily. "I'm not agreeing to anything until I hear more details."

"It's more fun when you argue with me," he complained.

"And I love pushing your buttons, but now is not the

time. We've already met up with one murdery monster. I'd rather not meet any more."

"Agreed." He pointed to a spot about half a kilometer to their right. "Hear that? I think that's our way down."

She went still and quiet, paling slightly. "Please tell me that's not a waterfall."

He caught her by the hand and set off toward the sound of rushing water. One way or another, he had to get Loris off this cliff and down to the river below. Something in his gut told him he was running out of time to get it done.

That morning, she'd woken up with more aches and pains than she could count, but she still felt better than she had in years. Fresh air, exercise, danger, and a hefty dose of mind-melting sex seemed to be the tonic she'd needed.

She'd looked at her wrists, admiring the markings in daylight for the first time. Whatever she had going on with Vengeance, it wasn't about sex. Well, not entirely. Was she really his mate? It seemed likely, but it was still hard to wrap her head around. They weren't even the same species. Had the verexi included enough human DNA in their creations make this bond possible? That didn't seem likely. She was no expert, but as far as she knew, none of the known species bonded like this.

Thoughts like this kept bouncing around her head as they made their way through the forest. She drank it all in, reveling in the wild beauty of this place. As they walked, Vengeance shared what he knew about the plants, the animals, and how they'd survived after the crash.

Sometimes she'd share stories about her experiences: the planets she'd seen while working as a bodyguard, the space stations she'd visited, and the various species she'd met.

By the time they'd reached the cliffs, she felt like they'd known each other far longer than a single day. He was a good male, one she was growing to like more and more.

Then he'd told her his plan, and she was back to thinking he was a cocky lunatic.

"Let me get this straight. Your plan is to use your netting to make a harness for me, and then you're going to lower me down the side of a waterfall that looks to be more than ten meters high and is surrounded by jagged, pointy rocks.

"There are areas where you can climb down yourself. I'll have hold of the rope to make sure you don't slip, but you'll be the one climbing."

"That's not much better," she said, already preparing herself for what she had to do. "And you still haven't told me how you plan to get yourself down."

"That's easy. I don't need the rope. I'll climb down freestyle."

She stared at him. "That's insane."

"The rope is too valuable to leave behind. We don't have much of it and no way to make any more. I'll be fine." He flashed her his trademark grin.

"Do not die on me, Venge. You can't just tell me I'm

yours, give me these damned tattoo things, and then do something stupid that gets you killed."

He took her hands in his. "I'm not going to die today. I have too much to live for."

He didn't so much make a harness out of the netting as wrap it around her torso until she felt like she was cocooned in the stuff. At least it wasn't bulky, but it restricted her range of motion more than she liked. Still, she'd make it work. She had to.

"Give me your bag," he said once she was ready. "I'll lower it down with mine before I make the climb myself."

She almost handed it over before she remembered what it contained. "The rifle stays with me."

He scowled but didn't argue.

She pressed the point anyway. "I'm not going down there unarmed. What if more of those black fangs are lurking around?"

He nodded. "Be careful. Not everything in these woods can be dropped with one shot. Don't start a fight you can't win."

It was good advice. "I won't." She drew out the rifle, snapped the two pieces into place, and slung it over her back. Then she kissed him, sinking into the warm comfort of his arms for as long as she dared.

"See you at the bottom. Stay safe."

"You too."

Once she started down, the noise would make it hard to hear anything he said, and the mist would keep her from seeing much. Every rock in view looked like it was covered in some kind of moss or algae, which meant everything would be slippery.

This was going to be *such* fun.

She was only two meters down when she heard it. That same deep, booming call. The pattern was identical. Two short beats followed by one long one. And it was getting louder.

Vengeance shouted to her, his voice barely carrying over the roar of the water. "Keep going. I'll get you down as far as I can before it gets here."

"No! Bring me back up! I can help!"

He ignored her and continued letting out the rope.

She reached the first stretch of climbable rocks and clambered down them as fast as she could manage. Sharp edges cut into her hands, but she kept going.

Three quick tugs let him know when she ran out of rocks to climb. To her relief, he took up the slack and began to lower her again, her feet dangling as she hung, helpless and frustrated, unable to see or hear anything.

She was part way down the second climbable section when the rope tightened. She tugged at it, but it didn't give. He must have tied it off.

"Vengeance!" she screamed his name. Not that it mattered. She couldn't help him.

Thud. Even this far down the waterfall, she felt the rocks around her shape as something huge approached from above.

Thud.

Thud.

Thud.

The next the booming roar was so loud it made the mist dance and whirl around her.

Angry tears scalded her cheeks as she started to climb

back up. It was pointless, but she did it anyway. If anything happened to him...

Pain twisted in her chest, and fear gathered in her throat, making it hard to breathe. Vengeance was up there alone. She should be with him. Fighting by his side. Keeping him alive, because if he died, she'd lose her only chance at love.

The word slammed into her like a comet strike. "Fuck me. I love him. He better not die, or I'll never get to tell him he was right."

She looked up again, and this time she saw him. He stood at the edge of the cliff, his sword in hand. He pounded a fist to his chest, striking the point where the markings intersected. Then he threw back his head and roared.

The beast roared back, and Vengeance vanished from sight.

She screamed his name, but she knew he wouldn't come back. He didn't have to. He'd already said goodbye.

12

For a moment, grief and fear paralyzed her, but it didn't last. She might not be able to help, but she could at least get ready in case an opportunity appeared.

She unslung her rifle and gave it a quick once-over to ensure nothing had happened to it during her climb. All good.

That settled, she shifted her stance until she was looking back up the way she'd come, her feet braced and most of her weight supported by the rope.

She could hear occasional roars over the waterfall, accompanied by loud thuds that sent random sprays of dirt and pebbles cascading off the cliff. Cursing, she turned away to protect her eyes and caught sight of something moving beneath her.

Shit. Now what?

A nightmare stalked the shore of the river below. The thing was *huge* with mottled yellow and gray scales and a tail so thick she couldn't have wrapped her arms around it. Massive jaws opened, revealing teeth like swords angled toward the back of the creature's mouth.

It stared at her with orange eyes. Still staring, it raised two surprisingly stubby arms and uttered an eerie trilling sound that drilled its way into her soul and booked an appointment to visit all her future nightmares.

Then it raised its head higher, and she realized it wasn't looking at her but at something happening *above* her.

She spun around in time to see Vengeance standing at the brink of the waterfall. His sword flashed, and something screamed in pain. Another slash and the water flowing past her changed color—first pink and then red. Blood. She leaned farther out, trying to get a better angle.

A shape charged into view. She recognized it as a larger version of the creature below.

Vengeance swung his sword again. She saw the blow land, cleaving deep into the monster's neck. *Yes!*

It staggered and dropped to its knees before vanishing from view again. The rocks shuddered around her. Was that it falling? Was the fight over?

The water was crimson now, and even the mist had turned a sickening shade of pink.

Her lover staggered into view at last. He raised a hand to her, and she waved back.

Then something struck him from behind. It whipped back and forth several times and then stopped. It didn't matter, though. The damage was done. Knocked off balance, Vengeance fell.

To Loris, it seemed as if the whole thing happened in

slow motion. She screamed and reached out as if she could somehow stop this from happening.

He managed to curl into a ball, his arms around his head as he plunged into the pool at the foot of the falls.

She had no idea how deep the water was. Could he survive that, or had his body shattered on rocks beneath the churning surface? She had no way to know.

She did know one thing, however. If she didn't kill the second creature, he *would* die. He'd been through too much to win another fight against a monster like that.

It stood in the same place it had been before, but something had changed. It took a moment for her to see it. The creature had puffed up its throat until it looked like it had swallowed a balloon. Then it raised its head and loosed a booming call that almost deafened her.

"Shut up!" she screamed as she raised the pulse rifle to her shoulder.

Still vocalizing, the beast broke into a run, its lower legs driving it forward at a terrifying speed. It was charging toward the pool, and she knew without looking what it was heading for.

Vengeance.

She pulled the trigger once, twice, three times. It kept running. Body shots weren't going to stop it. She paused, assessed, and chose a new target.

One leg buckled as an energy pulse shattered its knee joint. Did lizards have knees? She had no idea, but whatever she'd hit, it worked.

Once the creature was down, it was only a matter of time before she ended its life, but every second she had to focus on the monster was agony. She needed to get to Vengeance.

The second she was certain it was safe, she unclipped herself from the rope and started climbing down. By the time she reached the bottom, her hands were bloody and her pants were torn to shreds.

"Venge! You better not be dead!"

No answer. And no body. She didn't know if that was good or bad. She called out again as she splashed into the pool, trying to find him.

A golden blur moved from behind the waterfall. "I'm here."

He was alive. Thank the gods. Now she would not have to murder him for getting himself killed. The thought didn't make any sense, even to her, so she cast it aside and focused on reaching his side.

He looked rough. His nose was bloody, his face swollen, and one of his horns was broken. She stopped in front of him, afraid to hug him in case she caused him pain.

"I told you I didn't need the rope."

She gaped at him for a second, not sure if she wanted to laugh, cry, or yell at him. She threw herself into his arms and kissed him instead.

Then she shouted, "I thought I'd lost you before I could tell you I loved you. Don't you ever do that again!"

"Which part? Fight a thing we'll have to come up with a name for? Get knocked off a waterfall by the nameless thing's death throes? Or watch as my beautiful little warrior saved me from being eaten?"

"All of that!" she said. "And we're calling them boomers."

"Good name." He smiled at her, which only made his split lip bleed more.

Tears streamed down her face as she led him to dry land. Then she gave him her rifle while she treated the worst of his injuries with items from her personal medkit.

He kept touching her as if to reassure himself she was alright, and she never left his side for more than a second as she cleaned his wounds, regenerated the worst of the damage, and bandaged the rest.

He let her fuss over him, but the moment she was finished, he took charge again. "Sit."

"What? Why?"

"Because your hands are cut to ribbons. Show me how to use that regeneration thing you used on me."

She'd forgotten about her own injuries. Now that he pointed them out, the pain kicked in along with a heady sense of relief that unleashed a flood of tears.

"Damn it. You see what you made me do?" She held up one hand. "This is your fault, mister-I-don't-need-a-rope."

He kissed away her tears and then set to work patching her up. It didn't take long, which was a good thing. Other boomers could be around. Even if not, the scavengers would show up soon. Too much blood and death lingered in the air for them to ignore.

"I wish I could give you some pain killers, but I have no idea how the meds in that kit would react to your biology."

"I'll be fine. You're the one who needs something for pain." He pointed to the kit. "Which one do you need?"

She gestured to the vial she wanted. It was a mild pain killer that wouldn't muddle her mind too much. Even after her wounds were closed, her hands ached and tingled. New skin always did that, and she wouldn't be able to keep a tight grip on anything for at least a day.

When he was done treating her, he lifted her hands one at a time and gently kissed each finger followed by her palm. "I don't like that you were hurt trying to help me."

She leaned forward and kissed his still-swollen lips. "Right back at you."

"Let's get out of here. I have a good idea where we are now. There's a place we can rest about an hour's walk away. I've never seen one of the boomers before, so it should be safe."

She got to her feet, wincing as the newly healed skin on her legs pulled a bit. "That's good. But if we run across another one, we'll take it down together."

"Together," he agreed.

13

———

Vengeance had only found this place by chance, and he didn't get to visit often. It was too far away from his favored hunting grounds, but he liked it enough to come back now and then.

"Another waterfall? Aren't you tired of them after today?" Loris asked.

"This is only a tiny one," he said. "Please note the complete lack of boomers, black fangs, and anything else that might want to kill us."

"That is an improvement." Loris sighed tiredly. "And I could use a rest."

"So could I. In fact, I think we should plan to stay the night here. I've done it before. I even built a platform up in that tree."

She pretended to scowl. "Does this mean you're going to carry me again?

He managed not to grin as they fell into the now familiar pattern of teasing banter. "No need. It's got a ladder."

"This sounds better all the time. Show me?"

He shook his head. "First, we're going to get cleaned up."

She groaned. "More water?"

"Yes. But this water is warm. There's a hot spring nearby. I haven't found it yet, but enough of the hot water feeds into the stream to keep it a comfortable temperature."

"Warm water is a definite improvement. Tell me more."

He leaned in close and whispered in her ear. "I have soap in my bag."

She laughed in delight. "I'm sold on this idea. Bring on bath time!"

He led her to the water's edge and watched as she stripped off her clothes. The pants were in tatters, and blood stained her shirt. He'd have to ask Bysshe to make some new clothes for her. He had no idea what she'd want, but she'd only need them for the times they left his house. The rest of the time, he hoped she'd stay naked.

The soap was something they'd learned to make early in their time here. In the beginning they stayed inside the hull of their crashed ship. Sensitive noses and close quarters made cleanliness a requirement, especially for a group of males who could barely tolerate each other's company for more than a few hours at a time.

He handed Loris a small cake of soap. "I'll join you in a minute."

She nodded and stepped into the warm, welcoming waters. "Ooh, this is nice. I might float here for the next hour or so."

"I've done that before. It's so restful here I almost dozed off while I drifted around."

He set his sword near the water's edge and then took off everything he'd been wearing for the last few days. All of it went into the water. The leather was already wet, so another soaking wouldn't hurt. He used small handfuls of sand along with the soap to clean away the blood and dirt, and set it on some rocks to dry.

Then he sank into the heated water, letting it lap around his shoulders as he watched his mate scrub herself clean.

When she reached up to wash her hair, he moved to join her. "Let me."

She handed him the soap with a flourish. "Yes please."

They drifted together as he worked, his fingers massaging her scalp as he worked the suds into her hair. They didn't talk much. He sensed she didn't want that. She needed time to process everything they'd been through. So did he but not for the same reasons.

Facing death was nothing new for him. But today, he'd had someone else to fight for. And someone to live for.

He coaxed her to lie back so he could rinse the soap from her curls. She'd said she loved him. He knew what the word meant, but no one had ever said it to him before.

"I love you, little warrior." The words were strange on his tongue, but they felt right.

She turned and lifted her head to smile at him. "I know. I figured out your secret, Venge."

He looked at her in confusion. "What secret?"

She reached out and placed a hand on his chest, her palm centered over his heart. "When you say 'mine,' what you're really saying is that you love me."

He stared, too surprised to speak for several seconds. Then he laughed and drew her in for a long, heated kiss. "I didn't know that. But you're right." He nipped her lip between kisses. "Mine. Mine. Mine."

Her answering kiss was full of passion. "I love you, too."

They kept kissing as they drifted in the soothing water. He knew where he wanted to go, and she seemed content to let him take control. It wouldn't always be this way. Some days she'd fight him fang and claw. Other days she'd be as soft and gentle as a summer rain. Both were beautiful to him. However, he'd always love her best when she was at her fiercest. She was his little warrior, and she deserved the best life he could give her. Starting now.

They were almost to the waterfall by the time she raised her head to look at him. Her green eyes sparkled as she eyed the cascade of water. "We need to talk about this obsession of yours."

"Which one?" he asked.

"I was referring to your thing for waterfalls."

"So you're fine with my obsession with you?"

She wrapped her arms around his neck and kissed him until he'd nearly forgotten he'd asked her a question. Her tongue tangled with his, their breaths mingling as her soft curves pressed against his hard body and even harder cock.

Finally, she broke the kiss to answer him. "Your obsession with me is the most wonderful thing in all the worlds."

He drew her under the falling water, letting it pour over their heads like a massage from a hundred hands at once. He kissed her again, craving the taste of her mouth.

He couldn't hear her moan, but he felt it buzz against his tongue as he slid a hand between them. His fingers continued questing until they found the seam of her pussy. She responded by wrapping soft fingers around his cock. They teased each other until she was shaking, and he could hear his heart pounding even over the roar of the water.

He took her then, a simple matter of guiding her weightless body to the right spot. The warmth of the water gave way to the deeper heat of her pussy as he claimed her.

He moved them further under the overhang, turning so his back was to the falling water. When he found the rocky wall, he pinned her to it using the rocky floor to push himself even deeper.

She tangled her fingers in his hair and held on as he made love to her, every thrust stroking her inner walls and bringing her closer to release. The water stopped him from moving quickly, but the slower pace made everything more intense. The water swirled around them, adding new sensations to the moment.

The erotic dance continued with every step more

intense than the one before. He felt her moans against his lips as his cock began to thicken and twitch.

Her body tensed around him, milking his cock until he thought he'd die from the pleasure of it all. He tore his mouth from hers as an instinct he didn't understand forced him to drop his head to the crook of her neck. He bit her and felt her control snap a second later.

She came around him, her hands pulling on his hair as she drummed her heels into the small of his back.

Then it was his turn.

He emptied himself inside her, every jerk of his hips making her shudder and gasp. When his cock swelled up to lock them together, he raised his head and kissed her again.

He carried her back into the sunlight then. They floated like that for a long time. It was the most peaceful moment of his entire life, and Vengeance knew he'd never forget it. All his life, he'd wanted one thing that belonged to him and him alone.

He'd always wondered what it would be, and now he knew. It was the love of his little warrior.

14

A good night's rest and another soak in Vengeance's secret swimming hole made the last leg of their trek much easier.

Vengeance really did heal quickly. By the next morning the only injury she found was his broken horn.

"Are you sure it won't grow back?" she asked. Not that she cared about it. As far as she was concerned, it made him look even more wicked.

"I'm sure. But it's not a big deal. Honestly, none of us have been able to figure out why the scrawnies gave us horns at all. It's not like they're good for anything."

The opening was too good for her to resist. "Except as handles."

Her lover laughed. "True. I'll have to tell the others."

"No, you don't. Let them figure it out on their own."

They'd reached the well-maintained network of paths that linked the fa'rels' homes to each other and to the crash site where Bysshe resided.

Neither of them suggested going to Vengeance's

home first. If there was any news about the survivors, Bysshe was the one they should talk to.

Loris had come across a few androids, but they had all been basic models with little or no personality programs and only the most rudimentary functions. From what Vengeance had told her, Bysshe was quite different. As far as her lover was concerned, the android was family, and he'd played an important part in their lives.

The crash site looked like exactly what it was. The hulk of a large ship was partially buried by a landslide that must have happened when the ship had crashed into the side of a hill. A human-like figure with pale-blue skin was wandering around inside a fenced area, staring up at trees like the secrets to the universe were hidden somewhere in the branches.

"Is that Bysshe?" she asked.

Vengeance nodded. "It is. He's probably trying to estimate how much fruit is ready for picking and how many new trees we'll have to plant so all the humans will have enough to eat."

She'd been wondering about that. She had no idea what she could eat on this world. Since she'd been inoculated against most known pathogens, and parasites, she and Maddi weren't as vulnerable as some of the other women, but a poisonous berry would still kill them if they ate too many.

"You think some of this will be edible? Because I have to say, I'm getting a little sick of meal packs and ration bars."

"I'm sure of it. Though I'm not sure those fruit things

are an improvement over one of your meal packs. At least those have meat."

Huh. She hadn't considered Vengeance's diet. "You don't eat fruit?"

"No plants at all. Not unless it's been fermented into alcohol. The fa'rel are straight-up carnivores."

"You do realize that stuff in the meal packs is just cloned proteins in a sauce. Right?"

He shrugged. "Meat is meat."

Well, at least she wouldn't have to eat anymore salads. She was good with that. She wasn't fond of what one of her contracted guardians had called "rabbit food."

Vengeance called out to the blue-skinned android. He turned and actually smiled as he recognized him.

"You made it! If you were not back by this afternoon, I was going to send someone to look for you. Risk made it back with his mate late yesterday."

Vengeance looked confused. "They beat us back here? How?"

"They flew the shuttle. Risk nearly flattened part of my orchard when he landed, but he did quite well considering it was his first time. Please, do not tell him I said that."

"You said Risk returned with his mate. Do you mean Joy?" Loris asked.

Bysshe turned to look at her. "Joy Bashir. Yes. Ah. You also bear the mating marks. Congratulations to you both. You are Loris?"

"I am. It's nice to meet you, Bysshe."

The android smiled again. "The same to you. I am pleased you have arrived safely. You will be happy to hear that some of the passengers and crew of the *Harvest* survived the crash. We have only had one update, given the risk of anything we transmit being intercepted, but I thought you'd like to know what little news there was."

"That is great news! But where are Havoc and Maddison? You haven't mentioned them.

Bysshe lowered his head. She swore the android actually looked worried. "No one has heard from them."

No one said anything. "But you plan to send someone to look for them if they don't come back soon?"

"Yes. Mayhem and Strife have already volunteered. They are trying to convince their mates to stay behind."

"Who are their mates?" she asked, wanting confirmation of what she'd already heard.

"Mayhem is bonded to Bella, and Strife is with Rissa. They were both guests on the *Bountiful Harvest* but managed to make it to the escape pods before the ship crashed."

Loris recognized both names, but she hadn't spent much time with either woman. Still, she was happy to hear they were alive.

"Was your return home difficult?" Bysshe directed the question to Vengeance.

"We found a new creature we'll need to add to the threat list. Loris named them boomers. They appear to hunt in pairs and very nearly killed both of us. I'll give you a full report later." He paused and then added, "I assume Havoc and Joy had to fight off at least one ship's worth of mercenaries?"

Loris tensed. Vengeance had eventually told her about the ship he'd spotted at dawn the first day. While she understood why he hadn't told her, she was still grumpy about it.

"They did. What do you know?" Bysshe asked.

"Not much. I saw a ship flying low over the forest at dawn the first day after we parted ways with the others."

"Where were you when you saw it?"

Vengeance couldn't give anything like coordinates, but he managed to explain well enough that Bysshe nodded. "That's not good news. The mercenaries who went after Risk and Joy were already on the ground by the time the sun rose. That had to be a second ship."

Loris's heart sank. "Do you think they might have found Havoc and Maddison?"

"It's possible. But it's just as likely they will arrive here any minute, alive and well." Bysshe flashed a small smile at her. "Give them time."

"And until then, we should get some sleep." Vengeance gave her a meaningful look.

"Sleep. Right. I've been promised a comfortable bed in a tree house." She leaned in and whispered to Bysshe. "Is he telling the truth?"

"He is. You will be very comfortable here, Loris. If you wait a moment, I will gather up some fruits and vegetables for you to enjoy."

Vengeance sighed. "You keep your human food away from my nice, simple meat. Okay?"

"That's fine." She smiled at him, already this tree house of his. "I just have one more request."eager to see

"Anything you want, little warrior."

She slipped her hand into his and dropped her voice to a whisper. "Tell me who I belong to."

He flashed his fangs as he growled his answer. "You are *mine*."

Her heart swelled as she bumped him with her shoulder. "I love you too."

The End

✳✳✳

Thank You for Reading Marked For Vengeance

Want to read Venge and Loris's special bonus epilogue? Sign up for my newsletter here: subscribepage.io/Bonuscontent

Want to read more stories with book boyfriends
that are out of this world?

Check out Susan Hayes' other Science Fiction Romance
Series at
Susanhayes.ca

* 9 7 8 1 9 9 7 9 2 8 0 5 8 *